Dedicated to Mariette and Wayne...
I hope you will enjoy this adventure in memories.

Tibor Kamon

July 17, 2013

Find a place to call HOME

A Historical Nonfiction Novel

TIBOR KAMON

Order this book online at www.trafford.com
or email orders@trafford.com

Most Trafford titles are also available at major online book retailers.

© Copyright 2011, 2012 Tibor Kamon.

All rights reserved. No part of this publication may be reproduced, stored in a retrieval system, or transmitted, in any form or by any means, electronic, mechanical, photocopying, recording, or otherwise, without the written prior permission of the author.

Printed in the United States of America.

ISBN: 978-1-4669-2597-7 (sc)
ISBN: 978-1-4669-2596-0 (hc)
ISBN: 978-1-4669-2595-3 (e)

Library of Congress Control Number: 2012908708

Trafford rev. 05/25/2012

 www.trafford.com

North America & international
toll-free: 1 888 232 4444 (USA & Canada)
phone: 250 383 6864 ♦ fax: 812 355 4082

Office de la propriété intellectuelle du Canada
Un organisme d'Industrie Canada

Canadian Intellectual Property Office
An Agency of Industry Canada

Certificate of Registration of
Copyright

Certificat d'enregistrement du
Droit d'auteur

This Certificate of Registration is issued pursuant to sections 49 and 53 of the Copyright Act. The copyright in the work described below was registered on the date of registration as follows:

Ce certificat d'enregistrement est émis conformément aux articles 49 et 53 de la Loi sur le droit d'auteur. Le droit d'auteur sur l'oeuvre décrite ci-dessous, a été enregistré à la date d'enregistrement comme suit :

Date of Registration - Date d'enregistrement : **November 8, 2011**

Registration No. - Numéro d'enregistrement : **1091122**

First Publication - Première publication : **Unpublished**

Title - Titre : **Find a Place to Call Home**

Category - Catégorie : **Literary**

Owner(s) - Titulaire(s) : **Tibor G. Kamon**
6435 Nanaimo Street
Vancouver, British Columbia
Canada, V5P 4K9

Author(s) - Auteur(s) : **Tibor G. Kamon**

Date of Issuance of Certificate - Date d'émission du certificat : **November 8, 2011**

Registrar of Copyrights / Registraire des droits d'auteur
Copyright Office / Bureau du droit d'auteur

Canada

(CIPO 00200)
03-11

OPIC CIPO

CONTENTS

Chapter 1 What will happen to you now . . . ?........................ 1

Chapter 2 The Military Years... 9

Chapter 3 Early Days in Canada 26

Chapter 4 Fatal Attraction 42

Chapter 5 Montreal Expo 67 62

Chapter 6 East Africa 79

Chapter 7 Saudi Arabia 108

Chapter 8 Indonesia 136

Chapter 9 Summing Up 156

PREFACE

It is a question pondered by almost everyone somewhere along their life: "What is the purpose of my life on this earth?"

One of Hungary's great novelists Aron Tamasi had a very simple answer to this: "We have been put on this earth to find a place to call home."

When I thought about it, I realized just how true it is. Most of us will spend the greater part of our lifetime trying to find and establish a home, a place of safety and happiness.

It was this vision and my family and friend's encouragement that started me on the road to write this, somewhat personal historical novel of the Hungarian Revolution and the life and struggles of an immigrant. It may touch a cord in the hearts of many.

Memories are cherished secrets that we keep deep in our hearts. If we tell them, they cease to be memories.

—Joan Crawford

CHAPTER 1

What will happen to you now . . . ?

It was an unusually cool day for September in Hungary in 1937. A woman hurriedly walked from the bus station toward the hospital, holding the hands of two children. She was in her late thirties, still very pretty and well dressed, with striking brown eyes that sparkled. She ushered the two boys through the entrance of the hospital ahead of herself. The older boy was perhaps twelve, the other much younger, just approaching his third birthday. The boys were her sister's sons. The mother of the boys was the younger of the two sisters, and she had recently been involved in a bad accident. The cable of the elevator in her apartment building had broken and she had fallen four floors with it. She suffered internal injuries, and the rushed surgery that followed made things worse.

In the hospital, the younger sister knew she was dying. She had called her sister to bring the boys to her. She could never count much on her husband. He drove a taxi, but spent most of his days at the horse races. He saw a big win as the solution to all his financial troubles, but that big win never came. Often she had to borrow money from her sister to buy food. She knew that with her death, the family would fall apart and she wanted to ask her sister, who was still single and the godmother of the younger boy, to keep an eye on the children. She was all alone in the hospital room, propped up on a high pillow. Her face was pale, and she tried hard to suppress her pain. The two sisters were very much alike in their features; both were of dark complexion with deep brown sparkling eyes that made them so attractive.

When the boys entered the room with their aunt, they kissed their mother, which started tears in the corners of her eyes. She caressed the head of her younger son, then took his face in both hands, and the tears now flowed uncontrollably down her face as she repeated the words over and over again, "What will happen to you now . . . what will happen to you now?" The older boy had an inkling of what was happening, but the little one did not. He looked innocently at his mother and tried to smile. He had the good nature of his mother; he was always a pleasure to look after, always ready to smile. His eyes were the exact reflection of his mother's eyes.

Their mother's death and all the changes that followed confused the little three-year-old boy's whole existence. He hung onto his torn blanket for dear life as the only familiar thing that was left to him in his new environment. The father moved the family to a small one-bedroom flat to save money and have more left over to bet on the horses. The nearby grocer agreed to employ the older boy to help with deliveries before and after school time, which would help the family with the grocery bills. The boys' aunt came to feed the small child during her lunch-break from work; otherwise he was left on his own, alone in the apartment. He missed his mother's caressing and kissing the tip of his nose that was her custom in the mornings. He walked from room to room in the flat dragging his blanket behind him ceaselessly but never cried or emptied cupboards for something to do. He seemed to grasp that he should behave and not cause any trouble.

The two boys slept on the sofa bed in the living room and the young child sought comfort in holding onto his older brother's arm in his sleep. The twelve-year-old got up early every day and started delivery at six o'clock each morning before his school time at nine and again in the afternoon from three to six. He did his homework in the evening until sleepiness overtook him. He quickly took on the responsibility as the family provider and was very good with customers he delivered to, always ready to do little extras that endeared him to them. He received generous tips, and in less than a year, he had more money in his piggy bank than the father ever had in his bank account. The grocer's wife also rewarded him every day with leftover bread, fruits, vegetables, and meat that greatly lowered the household bill. The boy suggested to their father that they could buy a small flat of their own and he would contribute all his earnings toward the payments, but their father, never ready to handle financial commitments, refused.

The small child was also a major distraction for him, and he desperately sought ways to relieve himself of this responsibility. Finally he lucked out. The boy's grandparents (his parents) accepted custody of the child. They had just retired from their farm after fifty years of working the land and thought the little boy would bring them joy and would be better off being in their care.

Thus, the three-year-old found himself once again in a new environment, with seventy-year-old grandparents, in the small agricultural city of Bekescsaba, two hundred kilometers east of Budapest.

It would be twelve years before he saw his father and his brother again.

The two old people doted on the child, and he soon thought them to be his parents. He missed his mother's warmth and cuddling for some time, but the image faded more and more each year. The grandparents loved the child, but it was a different, less demonstrative love. The kisses, the warm embraces were not there. He was always well dressed and well fed, and there were several children of his age on the street to bond with. His friend's parents also treated him with special consideration. By the time he reached his sixth birthday, he was more than ready to enter elementary school. He already could read and played wicked chess games, thanks to the efforts of his closest playmate's father. He paid special attention to developing the boy's knowledge and character.

A favorite trick of the boys was to wait on the street corner for the girls of their age to come home with cans of drinking water, filled from the nearby artesian well, and then attack them in a mock Indian attack and empty the cans. But one day, they found their match in the sweet little six-year-old girl, who had enough of this injustice. She grabbed the two six-year-old boys by their ears and nearly tore them off. Blood was oozing down the faces of the two boys, and this alarmed the combatant little girl enough to forget her hard feelings and quickly bring them arm in arm to her mother for repairs.

This girl-boy fight was much discussed between them in between sweet kisses much later when they were thirteen years old. It was the year of sexual awakening, but in an innocent way. The two best friends were dating the same girl, taking her to the movies. One had his right hand on her left knee, the other his left hand on her right knee. Now and then, the two hands met in the middle.

The first year in school was coming to an early end. It was 1941, and Hungary was suddenly occupied by Hitler's Germany without much bloodshed. There were German soldiers everywhere; the elementary schools were closed and Hungary entered World War II as an ally of Germany. In the eyes of a six-year-old boy, the war was just a curious spectacle. Warplanes were flying over the city toward the frontlines, and they were bright objects in the sky to watch for and count them. At the nearby railway station, one could watch the railcars rolling by and count the number of tanks on them guarded by soldiers with guns, going somewhere who knows where or why. Then one bright sunny day, the planes unloaded their chain bombs. The target was the rail line, to stop the frontline supplies to the German troops. These were American planes. Everyone ran from the station to the bunker in the basement of the hotel across the street. The bombs missed the railway station and demolished the hotel with everyone in it. The newspapers headlined the next day that *'you are safest in the target area.*' The grandfather and the little boy were hit by the first airwave from the explosion in the supply room where the glass preserve bottles were crashing down on the floor, but without breaking on the dirt floor. They were thrown against a flour sack that opened up spewing white flour at the two, one so young and the other so old. They looked at each other with bewilderment like two circus clowns, but their faces closer to tears than laughter. From then on Grandma sent the little boy out to the farm for safety. After two weeks she sent Grandpa to bring him home. That night they were bombed again.

Years later the German troops were in retreat to the west toward Budapest, and Russian troops rolled in. The difference between the two armies was that the retreating German soldiers paid with valueless German currency for anything they confiscated while the Russian soldiers simply confiscated everything. The grandfather decided to welcome a small Russian tank brigade on the farm, his reasoning being that the army personnel might spare his livestock and confiscate chickens and ducks from the neighboring farms. The troops prepared their meal in a huge copper kettle over an open fire, borscht with everything in it but the feathers. But they were ordered to move on before the soup was eaten. The grandfather was left with the biggest bowl of soup of his life. He quickly called over all his neighbors to share in the feast, knowing full well where the raw materials came from.

The Russian troops moved quickly through the eastern rural areas of Hungary in the fall of 1944. The main defense-line was set up by the German army around the capital city of Budapest and on the western side of the Danube.

What the ten-year-old boy did not know was that his brother, now nineteen, had been drafted by the Hungarian Armed Forces and was part of this defense line. They were deployed on the eastern side of the Danube River, to protect the German retreat on the western side toward Austria, in case the Russian troops succeeded crossing the river. The brigade commander of this Hungarian contingent was fully aware that the war was lost and was not ready to sacrifice any of his men. He instructed his soldiers to hold their fire and be prepared to surrender. It was the first Hungarian brigade to surrender, and their example was quickly followed by the rest of the Hungarian army. The brigade commander was loath to throw away his leather coat despite warnings from fellow soldiers and was mistakenly taken for a German officer and was shot. He succeeded in protecting his troops, but lost his own life on account of a leather coat.

In the first election in Hungary after the war in 1945, the socialist Social Democratic Party won the majority of seats, and the Communist Party, despite the presence of occupying Russian troops, came in a distant second. This did not please the Kremlin much, and in 1949, the Social Democratic Party was forced into a merger with the Communist Party, and slowly, as the socialists were forced to step down or were murdered, Hungary became a Russian satellite firmly controlled by the Communist Party. Members of the prewar Hungarian army brigade that had been the first to surrender to the Russians were given medallions for bravery by the communist government. Whether you are labeled a coward or a hero really depends on circumstances and who won the war.

It did not matter much to the nineteen-year-old; he was just happy to be alive. With some help from his medallion for bravery, he secured a job with the Hungarian Post & Telecom and soon married the girl with the most attractive smile in the telegraph office, who was his age. To marry right after the war was no small undertaking. Many of the buildings in the city were heavily damaged in bombing raids, and apartments were impossible to get. The newly weds moved in with the bride's parents in a small one-bedroom flat. It took nearly four years before they were able to afford their own apartment, by which time relations with the parents were stretched to the breaking point.

The rural areas of Hungary did not suffer much from the war, but the political changes occurring after the war soon wreaked havoc with the farming community. Farms greater than a housing plot were confiscated by the Communist government and were integrated into communes. The boys' grandparents lost their farm and their income from it. They were reduced to near poverty after working the land for fifty years. They still had their garden home in town, and they made the best of the new reality of life, growing fruits, potatoes, and vegetables in the garden and raising a pig each year in the back livestock pen. This is how most of the rural area people survived.

The younger boy was now nearly fifteen years old, and one day, on a sudden impulse, got on his bicycle and cycled to Budapest looking for his brother and father. He arrived at his brother's flat in the late evening, exhausted and suffering from a mild sun stroke. His brother was still living with his wife's parents, and accommodating him here was impossible. Their father lived in a one-room rented flat with no place for his young son there either.

So his father, through his contacts at City Hall, where he was a part-time night watchman, arranged for the boy to be put up at the live-in school for orphan children that was run by the municipality. The fifteen-year-old spent two years in the orphanage, all the time desperately wanting to get out of there. One day, he noticed a billboard invitation to enter the Air Force Academy and train to become a fighter pilot. Without giving any thought to what it meant to be in the military, he sent off his application, and at the age of seventeen, was accepted by the Academy. He graduated from the school with honors at age nineteen as a two-star lieutenant. The older brother had graduated from night school classes as an accountant, and now both men were earning a living. The two had always had a strong underlying belief that their mother was protecting them with invisible arms from above, and it was probably true.

CHAPTER 2

The Military Years

The nineteen-year-old lieutenant's first posting was the air force base outside the city of Kaposvar at the Taszar air base, in southwestern Hungary. It was the base for three squadrons of aged, propeller driven Soviet fighter aircraft. The Russian military had a long-established policy to sell their retired and outdated aircraft to their satellite communist states in exchange for valuable resources and industrial and agricultural products.

He was given command of the technical staff maintaining the aircraft's instrumentation and communication equipment. Meals for officers were served in the officer's mess, and he soon noticed that socialism does not necessarily mean equality. The pilots were served separately, and they were served more nutritious meals; they had chocolate milk for breakfast. He was fond of chocolate milk, but the technical staff was never served any. This was his first disappointment with being mildly cross-eyed and as a result having been rejected during medical examinations to qualify as a pilot. He didn't know that he was very lucky to be accepted into the ranks as anything at all. The political commissar at the academy had discovered that he had been brought up by his grandparents, who were rich landowners and he therefore had been categorized as '*not working class.*' That their land was confiscated, and they were dead didn't seem to matter. (His grandparents died during his first year at the Academy.) Unknown to him, only the intervention of the class secret political watchdog saved him, who reported on him favorably, and he was also the Academy's top student.

A pilot's performance in the air during exercises depended heavily on the communication equipment, and our lieutenant was often asked to fly in the gunner's back seat if an equipment problem persisted. For his brave co-operation he soon had access to all the chocolate milk he ever wanted to drink as he became a close friend of the pilots. He didn't realize just how much danger he was in during these flights as he had never parachuted from an aircraft.

On one occasion, the base commander had complained that voice communication with his gunner was intermittent in flights. Our lieutenant readily volunteered to fly with the base commander and donned a parachute. He was given a short demonstration regarding how to operate it. In flight he soon located the cause of the problem, a loose wire connection. But midway into their flight they were facing a much bigger problem. The motor started sputtering, and smoke was rising from the engine. The voice of the commander came over the repaired intercom: "On your left is a red ejection enabler, should it become necessary. Do not panic, just open the parachute as I taught you, shortly after being thrown. But I will attempt to land the aircraft."

His commander's calm voice washed away his fears and he watched the smoking engine with curious eyes as the aircraft was approaching the runway. It all ended well with the burning oil being quickly put out as the plane came to a halt. Our lieutenant was cited for action beyond call of duty. But he never again volunteered to fly and was glad he had failed the medical to become a pilot. He really didn't have a military aptitude in his makeup and ending up in the military was merely the result of not having a home.

The fighter pilots at the base were truly a special breed. They were exceptionally brave, with a strong hint of showmanship and swaggering. To be the best overrode everything else. During exercises to pull up from a dive, with their lungs in their throat, and then disappear in the clouds from their pursuer and to reappear on the tail of their fellow pilot with a chuckle was magical potion.

They didn't read Tolstoy or poetry. For them art existed only in the sky, in the clouds, in speed, in acceleration, and quickness of reaction. Although basically they were trained to kill, it had not really entered their minds. It was not a reality like it would be for a foot-soldier bayoneting the enemy. It was something far away, not visible, much like dropping bombs in target practices. But in their everyday life, they lived only for today, with a lingering undercurrent that tomorrow may not be theirs. At this base this superstition was especially strong as the crash rate was very high with these outdated aircraft. On weekends they changed into civilian clothes and partied late into the night. They were a wild bunch and foolishly generous, and the women of Kaposvar loved them.

It was our lieutenant's twentieth birthday when a group of pilots dragged him to town to celebrate. He was shy with women and wasn't much of a drinker either. The pilots had a prearranged plan for him, but it wasn't the girl they chose for him that approached him for the first dance but a woman in short polka-dot dress sitting with three other women at a corner table by the orchestra. She was older, probably closer to thirty than twenty. She was straight forward in what she wanted, and before the pilots could have their way to execute their plan, the two were out on the street, on their way to her apartment.

She showed him the bathroom and told him: "Have a shower and I will join you in a minute."

She entered the shower naked. This was the first time our lieutenant had seen a woman completely disrobed. She massaged him gently with soap where he was most sensitive, and it evoked a rise almost instantly. She led him to the bedroom, whispering: "Don't rush, hold back, please."

But he was inexperienced and awkward. He was cut sharply and was bleeding profusely.

"I am sorry, it should be me bleeding, not you, my dove" she said.

She bandaged him gently and released him back to the base with a kiss. She was careful not to discourage her young lover.

He entered the city hospital early the next morning somewhat embarrassed. A young nurse, probably his age, asked the questions:

"What is your name?" He told her.

"What is your address?"

"I am from the Air Force base."

"Oh, you are military?"

"Yes."

"They have their own medical center at the base, why are you checking in here?"

"Well, it is kind of embarrassing, I am cut badly, and it is very painful."

"What is painful? Where are you cut?"

"Here." He pointed to his groin.

"Let me see."

"Here?"

"OK, come with me," she said and closed the curtains around a bed.

"How did this happen?"

"Well, it happened while . . ."

"All right, you don't have to explain. We have to check you in for a few days. You will have to be circumcised. You are lucky it didn't get infected."

He got a private room, and after changing, was wheeled into the operating room immediately. They obviously took his situation seriously.

It was quickly over, and his penis was sewn up in a neat circular bouquet.

And if he thought he was in pain before, he had no idea what was coming. It was another young nurse that looked after him in recovery. She was pretty and coquettish. She enjoyed teasing him.

She lifted the blanket and giggled: "Now, let us see what we have here. He sure looks withered. But don't worry, in a couple days it will be playful again." She covered him up and danced out of the room.

The night visit got a little bit more embarrassing. She not only uncovered him and looked but touched him and examined the threaded area. The rise was instantaneous and the pain was excruciating. The thin thread was cutting into the sensitive skin like a knife.

This must be worse than childbirth, he thought.

She just laughed.

"You are doing marvelously. He is obviously back to life already."

It was five days of repeated coquettish torture until the thread was removed.

When he was leaving the hospital he turned to the nurse:

"You can touch me now. I feel no pain."

"I would love to," she said. "But I am married already."

Walking away from the hospital he looked back and thought: *My mother should have had me circumcised when I was a child. But at the Turkish baths, now they will think I am Jewish.*

He didn't have a chance to try the role of a lover again. He was selected with nine others from his graduating class to go for six months training in Russia on maintenance of MIG-15 aircraft that the base would soon be receiving. Within a week, they were on the train en route to somewhere east of Moscow. The location was kept secret from them. The train ride was long and boring, and somewhere in the Ukraine our lieutenant, along with another thirsty friend, got off the train when it stopped at a station. Getting off the train was prohibited, but they didn't take this prohibition too seriously. It took them far too long to find the old peasant woman selling bottled drinks and even longer to understand how much they owed her. Without them noticing it, the train left and they were standing baffled somewhere in the middle of the Ukraine with very little knowledge of Russian.

Very quickly they were arrested by the station master and a very stern-looking armed man as foreign spies and were locked up in a small backroom. But luckily it didn't take long before a call was received by the station master telling him that two Hungarian officers were missing from the train. He beckoned the waiting taxi in front of the station and told the driver to catch up to the train. And catch up he did, going at one hundred kilometers per hour on dirt road. The dust raised was probably visible on radar screens across half of the Ukraine. The two were eased out of a considerable sum of rubles and were severely reprimanded, but that was easier to get over than being locked up as spies in Allied uniform.

The rest of the trip was uneventful, and they arrived at the secret Russian air base all together. It was cold; winter was in the air already in early October. They were assigned rooms in a special barrack that contained classrooms as well as living quarters and common washroom and exercise facilities. It was located next to the base commander's house on the edge of the forest surrounding the base. The commander was an elderly man; he must have been closer to seventy than sixty. He was up at six o'clock every morning jogging around the base in a T-shirt and shorts in the dead of winter. After the first day of introduction to the teaching staff and class rooms, four weeks were dedicated to learning the Russian language. Our lieutenant learned the language quickly. He had an advantage in that his grandparents spoke Slavic in the house when he was a child, and Russian being a Slavic language came easily to him. He was often used as interpreter for the struggling students. After four weeks of language course, the technical training was conducted in Russian. It was amazing how fast they could learn the language when forced into it.

The base commander's house had another attraction besides the old general running in T-shirt and shorts in -20 degrees Celsius temperatures. An attractive woman maybe thirty years old, in a long flowing dress and high red boots, swept the back balcony of the drifted-in snow every afternoon. Her hips moved rhythmically with each sweeping motion, almost deliberately, invitingly. Our lieutenant was sure she did it on purpose. During breaks between classes he walked out between the two buildings to a path in the forest and watched her. One day, the woman followed him. She was covered in a long mink overcoat. The path was narrow and when he turned they came face to face. She had shining bright eyes that were just as inviting as the rhythm of her walk. She opened the furry coat and embraced him. He kissed her. He had to rush back to class and asked if he could see her again. She just nodded and said: "Da."

He was so proud of himself he boasted to everybody about his quick conquest. But the group leader, who was from the Hungarian ministry, wasn't impressed.

"Do you know who that woman is?" he asked, alarmed.

"She wore a mink coat. She is not the maid, I am sure of that. Maybe she is the commander's daughter," he replied.

"No, she is the base commander's wife."

He knew at that instant that he could not be a lover to this attractive Russian woman in the snow on a mink coat no matter how much longing he had for it.

That was the end of his Russian romance, and for the next five months he fought the desire to walk the forest path. His heroism did show up in his marks; they were assessed as '*Outstanding*.'

During these six months, the Hungarian technical staff all received their salaries in rubles and had no place to spend them. So they all purchased motorcycles, which were the best value for the money, to take home. It afforded a much envied freedom for trips to Kaposvar and for excursions to Europe's largest lake, Lake Balaton, when the lieutenant returned to Hungary.

On return from Russia it was a relief to be home in Taszar, back among his beloved pilots, who now flew the newly arrived MIG-15 fighter planes. These planes proved to be just as dangerous to fly as the earlier propeller-driven aircrafts and they soon earned the nickname *the flying coffins*. Today a visitor to the airfield would find a MIG-21 displayed in front of the Education Building and the name plates of fifteen pilots under the wings who lost their lives during flight exercises. The airfield itself had a tumultuous history. During the Hungarian revolution in 1956 it was the first airfield encircled by a Russian tank brigade to prevent any aircraft from becoming airborne. After the collapse of communism, in 1995 during the Balkan war it became an American air base for bombing raids on Serbia, and in 2002 for bombing raids on Iraq.

In 1955 it was simply home for the Hungarian Fiftieth Fighter Regiment. And the pilots were happy to see their lieutenant they fondly called '*Chocolate Milk*' back in their midst. They knew that with him around their pride and joy, their aircraft, would be conscientiously looked after. And now they were ready to redeploy their plan that had been put on ice for a year. On his twenty-first birthday, they dragged him once again to their favorite bar and dance hall, and this time, made sure he had the first dance with the right girl. Her name was Marika Hortobagyi.

"You were supposed to dance with me last year," she said. "But you took off with that polka-dot dame."

"Who said I was supposed to dance with you?"

"It was your squadron commander. He dropped me. He found a new girlfriend. He promised he would find someone for me, someone better than him. He's tried to lure me back since, but I have refused him."

"So, am I better?"

"I don't know yet, but you dance better. I am so glad you are not a pilot."

This is just the way of these pilots. Life and love is for today. They have no thought of tomorrow, he thought.

Marika had deep brown, trusting eyes and simple straight forward manner. *She reminds me of my mother,* he thought. She had no pretensions. She was an exquisite dancer and the two of them had a trusting intimacy right away, as if they had known each other for years. She had a beautiful sporty figure. She was light in steps; dancing with her was almost like floating on air. She didn't have the classical lines of beauty in her face, but it was warm, open, inviting, gentle, and trusting. And her eyes shone with a twinkling delight. Her voice was warm and soothing, almost musical. She agreed to meet him again the next weekend for a motorcycle ride to Keszthely on the south shore of Lake Balaton. It had a world-famous castle, the Festetics Castle, and her married sister lived there. And only six kilometers from Keszthely lay the Heviz hot springs.

"We can stay at the hot springs, if you like and just drop in to visit my sister," she said. These words were simple, but they promised much, and he looked forward to the weekend with excitement.

When they got to Keszthely, Marika changed her mind.

"Let us just go on to the hot springs. We can visit my sister another time."

Our lieutenant was more than pleased with this turn of events, and the motorcycle willingly made the turn onto the road to Heviz. She clutched him tighter from behind.

The Heviz hot springs is actually a lake, bearing the same name as the town. It is a unique thermal lake with a surface area of close to five hectares, covered with water lilies and in places it reaches depths of thirty meters. It is the second largest hot-water lake in the world with a temperature around thirty degrees Celsius. It was a spa dating back to Roman times. Roman coins were discovered at the bottom of the lake. When the wooden changing cabins in the middle of the lake came into view, Marika exclaimed excitedly: "It is so beautiful, let's go swimming now."

"We should find a place to stay first before they are all taken" and he gently touched her leg. It was early autumn, and her body exuded warmth despite the cooling breeze of the ride.

They were lucky to find a little cottage on the first turn with a sign: *'Bed and breakfast.'*

"I love it. It looks like a house in Switzerland with the geraniums in the window," Marika exclaimed, brushing his back with her face.

The proprietor was an elderly lady with a big smile. She had a practiced eye to spot lovers, and she had a special chamber in her heart for them. She knew how to make them feel at ease and welcome.

"This way, I have a special room for you." She guided them to the back of the house. The room was small, but it was very clean and had a bathroom with a shower. The window looked toward the lake.

"Breakfast will be served in the kitchen in the morning at seven. There is just one more couple in the house. Feel at home and enjoy your stay. Oh, you look so lovely together," she sighed, and turned with a smile.

That night and the year that followed was the happiest time in the life of our lieutenant. Lovemaking with Marika was an intoxicating experience. It engulfed his whole being in ecstasy. It was like something one experiences when listening to a beautiful melody the first time. Her demonstrative unrestrained love reminded him of just how much he had lost with the early death of his mother. Being in love and being with Marika was home, what he had longed for all this time, and he wanted to spend the rest of his life with her.

Then, history took an unexpected turn. In 1956, there were signs of simmering unrest in the capital, Budapest. The Writers Union openly criticized government policies that were dictated from Moscow and demanded the exit of Hungary from the Warsaw Pact. Imre Nagy, the newly reinstated Prime Minister of Hungary, was sympathetic to the aspirations of the nation but was reluctant to invoke the anger of the Soviet Union. An ultimatum came quickly from Nikita Khrushchev's government to crush this newest threat to the rule from Moscow. The Hungarian government in turn demanded that Russian troops leave the country. The Russians appeared to oblige and started moving their troops out. But at the same time, they were moving new troops in from Siberia and performed a troop rotation under the pretext of moving their troops out. Overnight the base at Taszar was surrounded by a Russian tank regiment. The base commander was ordered to assemble all Hungarians at the base and send them home.

Our lieutenant was wondering where that home was for him. He got on his motorcycle with a classmate from the Academy and the two of them rode toward Budapest. His friend had a married sister who lived in Budapest in an apartment. Her husband was an officer with an artillery brigade, which had been deployed on the east side of the city on two sides of the main road, to blockade any attempted Russian troop entry.

At this time, there were not many troops visible yet in the countryside. They met just one busload of Hungarian soldiers with machine guns.

"The Russians surrounded the Taszar air-base," our lieutenant shouted at the truck load of troops. "We should fight them."

One soldier unhooked his machine gun and threw it at him, which he just managed to grab by the shoulder strap.

"You go and fight them!"

And there they were, two air force officers with a machine gun on a motorcycle, to fight the Russian army. At a nearby apple orchard, the owner saw the episode and waved frantically for them to come in.

"You are fools; you will be killed with that gun in your hand. Give it to me I will hide it." He probably saved their lives with that gesture.

As they got close to Budapest, they started to realize the true extent of the devastation the city had suffered. Hundreds of Soviet tanks had invaded the city, and they had fired at everything indiscriminately. It was November 10, 1956 and the city was under Soviet occupation. The people were overtaken by fear. His friend's sister, Anna, and her husband, Bela, were home and packing, and she looked at them in surprise.

"How on earth did you manage to get into the city?"

"We met no opposition," they tried to humor her.

"This is no time for joking. There is an arrest warrant out for Bela. He gave the order to fire on the Russian troops. We are leaving for the Austrian border. We have been given the address of a contact in Sopron, who would guide us to the border. What are you two planning to do?"

The two friends looked at each other and winced.

"We will join you. What else can we do? Do you have a car?"

"Yes, we have a Trabant. We have to hurry before the border gets sealed off. Do you know a way to get us to Sopron?" she asked.

"Yes. We will drive south and then west, avoiding the larger cities and military bases that may be under Russian occupation already. But I wish I could talk with my brother and Marika before I do this," our lieutenant burst out.

"There is no time for that. We have to leave right away," she said.

And the four of them had left with nothing more than the clothes on their back and what money they had. They arrived in Sopron at the given address before sunset. A man perhaps fifty years old in high boots greeted them and informed them that they would start out as soon as it turned dark.

"You will have to leave the car and the motorcycle here," he said.

There were four other people at the farmhouse already, who would be joining them. They were somewhat alarmed at the prospect of so many people, which could make crossing the border undetected so much more difficult. But they were in no position to argue; they paid the fees demanded and followed the man through the heavily treed forest, sweating in their many layers of clothing and stumbling on the underbrush. After about an hour's walk the man pointed ahead to a hill and said: "The border is just beyond that hill: You can't miss it from here."

And with that, he turned and left them. But the hill was farther than it looked, and the women of the other group started to complain loudly. Before they realized it, they were surrounded by German shepherds dogs and border guards.

The bastard delivered us to a guard station deliberately, they thought. They were led to a fairly large building where thirty to forty people were held already, waiting for questioning. There were three rooms in all, and an armed guard stood in front of each door. One room held those waiting to be questioned, and another was for those who had been questioned already and had been released. The third was the interrogation room. From here people were either released or arrested. It was Bela, the artillery officer, who was interrogated first and he was not released. The two air force officers would have been next, and they knew they were in serious trouble. Anna saw her husband taken away, and now, she feared for her brother. She approached the guard and pleaded with him. He motioned behind his back and let the two men slip across to the other room.

There is nothing like the influence of a beautiful woman, they thought. Later they were escorted to the nearby railway station and were given a lecture on not trying this again.

"Next time we will not be so generous," they were told.

On the train, it was quiet in the compartment except for the clattering of the wheels, and their concern was palpable. *What will happen with Bela? Will they jail him? Will they execute him?*

They don't have a record on me, thought our Lieutenant. *Maybe I can return to the base. It just wasn't meant for me to emigrate. What would I do in a foreign world without Marika anyway? I need my motorcycle back.* All kinds of thoughts were swiftly racing through his mind.

Back in Budapest, he discussed these things with his brother.

"The situation is ugly here. I wish you had succeeded leaving the country," was his brother's assessment.

"What about Marika?" he asked.

"Ask her to go with you. You are both young. You can create a life for yourself in a free country, perhaps Canada. I can arrange a work permit for you for employment with the Post and Telecom in Sopron, and that will allow you to travel by train through the restricted Western zone. The authorities are trying to shut down the outpouring of refugees and created a restricted travel zone on the border with Austria."

He telephoned Marika, but it was her father who answered the phone:

"Marika was killed by a Russian soldier, who tried to rape her and she resisted," said the sobbing voice from the other end.

"No!" cried out our lieutenant, and the phone fell from his hand. He covered his face, and his whole body was shaking with indescribable pain.

"Going back to Taszar has no meaning for me now. Without Marika it would no longer be home. I will try again to cross the border and this time I will succeed. I will go alone," he said, wiping the tears that were streaming down his face.

His brother embraced him, trying to console him.

"These bastards claim to be our friends! Imagine if they came as our enemies," our lieutenant sobbed.

The next day, he boarded the train for Sopron. At the first station in the security zone, soldiers with machine guns boarded the train and checked everyone's ID. The official employment letter was scrutinized, and although there was some hesitation, it satisfied them.

The next day, he reported at the Post and Telecom office in Sopron and was designated as assistant cable splicer; he carried the ladder to get down into the manholes.

"You would think they had ladders permanently installed in the manholes," was his first comment under the weight of the ladder.

"In any decent country that would be the case, but not here," replied the technician. "We don't have any instruments to detect gas leaks either. I have to rely on my nose. I always throw a match in first just to be sure. We know you won't be with us very long. You were assigned to me to protect you and guide you. Actually getting across the border is quite simple. Just follow the railway line to Austria. You could start tomorrow night if you want to."

The next night, he dressed warmly and started walking along the railway line. He was sweating heavily under the many layers of clothing, his boots were heavy with mud, and his heart was beating furiously. After walking several hours, he caught sight of a guard tower that seemed unattended. Still, he decided to be cautious and crawled along the ground as they had taught him at the Academy until the tower was well behind him. He was now sure that he was across the border and decided to walk on the rail line timbers. He came to a station with low light and a man holding a lantern on the platform. He asked him, "Austria?"

The man holding the lantern replied with an accent, "Austria."

With a sigh of relief, he pulled out all his Hungarian paper money and showed it to the station master, who walked to his ticket office and returned with Austrian schillings. It was an exchange of currency well below the official exchange rate, but it was probably enough for a ticket to Vienna. The lieutenant was told that the next train would be arriving from Hungary in about two hours and would continue on to Vienna.

When the train arrived, he was escorted by the station master to a coach that was fairly full. "It is cheaper," he was told. He sat down on the wooden bench across from a couple in their thirties. They smiled at him and asked him something that he didn't understand. He just waved his hands and smiled back. The woman had sandwiches on her lap on a paper towel and offered him one. He took it and ate it with gusto; he hadn't eaten since he left Sopron. They offered him a banana next. This was a fruit our lieutenant was not familiar with. Tropical fruits were not available in Hungary in those days. He bit into it without peeling it. The couple laughed and peeled it for him. It created a warm feeling between them. When the ticketing officer walked by their bench and asked for his ticket, he pulled out all his schillings and gave the whole amount to him. The ticket officer started counting it, but the passengers began booing him loudly. He looked around, threw up his hands, and returned the money. Austrians themselves had been under Russian occupation not that long ago, and they understood what Hungarians were going through.

It was early morning when the train arrived in Vienna. The Austrian couple with gestures and drawings asked our lieutenant if he had a place to go.

He shook his head.

They gestured to him to follow them. The man entered a phone booth and made several phone calls.

Stepping out the booth he drew a picture of a school building and asked the lieutenant if he was a student.

He said, "Yes." And that wasn't a lie as he did finish first year of engineering by correspondence that year, paid for by the military.

They called a taxi and took him to a place that turned out to be special campus for students that was funded by the World Student Organization. This turned out to be a great stroke of luck for him as all Western nations were eager to bring the university graduates to their country first, ahead of other refugees. In the office where he had to sign in, they asked him which country he preferred, and he remembered his brother's advice as he wrote down Canada. Under military service in the questionnaire he stated that he was an air force lieutenant and served at the Taszar base. The next day, two dour-looking men in military uniform showed up at the campus and requested to see our lieutenant. The interview was conducted in a private room, and the two men asked him all kinds of questions about the air base and the weaponry on the MIG-15 jets. They also asked him if he intended to stay in Austria.

He told them he had applied for immigration to Canada. This seemed to satisfy them and they left. Our lieutenant thought: *How strange it is, in Hungary the authorities distrusted me because I was not 'working class' and here they distrust me because I might be a Communist and possibly a spy. What will they think of me in Canada? All I want in this whole wide world is just a place to call home.*

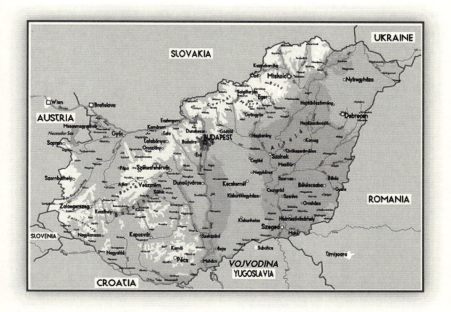

CHAPTER 3

Early Days in Canada

Selecting Canada as their destination turned out to be a great choice for all the Hungarian students who applied, close to six hundred. Among them the entire school of forestry from Sopron that included students and teaching staff. The government of Canada was quick and efficient in processing such a large group of people. They had promised the students that they will be in Canada within two weeks and they kept that promise. Three large military aircraft picked up the students from Vienna and brought them to McGill University in Montreal in a single operation.

As the planes were on their final approach to Montreal airport all eyes were on the ground below and they could hardly believe what they saw: parking lots full of automobiles, cars everywhere. *Can we own an automobile someday?* they wondered.

From the airport, they were transported on buses that formed a long lineup at the airport terminal to the student cafeteria at McGill. Here everything was ready to treat six hundred Hungarian students to their first Canadian meal. And it was the best their Canadian hosts could think up: Alberta beef, rare, barbecued to perfection with baked potatoes and sour cream.

So why were so many leaving their steaks untouched? The staff was bewildered. *What is wrong?*

Well, nothing was wrong. But Hungarians do not normally eat meat that squirts blood. Once the problem was grasped, the chefs with great consternation ruined the steaks to '*well done.*'

The students were housed in various dormitories on campus and outside the campus. Representatives from Universities across Canada came and interviewed potential candidates to bring them to their school. The professor from University of Alberta spoke Russian and as this was someone our lieutenant could converse with, he signed up. Twenty five others did the same and within a few days they were enjoying a four day train ride to Edmonton, Alberta. Our lieutenant was attracted to two students in the group who talked as if they had known each other in Hungary already. It turned out that they had known each other from early childhood and crossed the border together. He quickly warmed up to them and enjoyed their cheerfulness and friendly attitude with delight. He no longer felt alone in a foreign land.

By the time they arrived in Edmonton, he came down with a fever and was taken to the University hospital straight from the railway station. It turned out to be a strep throat and he was put on antibiotics for a week. His new friends, Paul and Miki, visited him every day, and this strengthened the bond between them. It was the beginning of a friendship that would last a life time.

The Hungarian students were housed at the University of Alberta dormitories and were given English lessons for a month. It was early May now and the end of the school year, and the regular students were leaving the residences for summer vacation.

The University was very generous with the Hungarian students. It provided housing for them in the residences for the summer and for the school year following, free of charge, and their tuition fees in their first year were also paid for by the University. They quickly came to the realization that they may just have made the best choice back in Montreal.

It was now time to look for summer jobs with the little English knowledge they possessed. Here our lieutenant lucked out in a monumental way. Another student who had been hired for a surveying job with the Department of Transport told him that those people were also looking for someone with radio knowledge. He applied the next morning and was hired. And he had a summer job for the next four years.

The first two weeks he was told to read and learn English.

"Go out and find for yourself a book to read," the department head told him.

In the first bookstore, he found one with an attractive woman on the cover page and brought it to the office with excitement. But there were words in this book he had difficulty finding in the dictionary. He asked the department's secretary, a young woman his age, what was meant by the line in the book: "He farted and his ass was black with soot."

"What on earth are you reading?" she asked him and burst into a loud giggle.

"Peyton Place," he said.

"We better get you another book," and the next day she brought him Tolstoy's *War and Peace*.

"Have a memorable summer," she said.

He had been assigned to work with Lofty, an elderly technician, who was approaching sixty-five and was retiring that year. The two of them would spend four months together at the Aishihik airport at the north end of Aishihik Lake in the Yukon Territories. They couldn't have chosen a better man to teach our lieutenant the English language. Lofty was well known for his flowery expressions. Lofty was also very vocal when he worked and our lieutenant was in for a treat.

Lofty told him that they will be installing and putting into operation VOR navigational aids. The VOR is a Very High Frequency (VHF) Omnidirectional Range. It is a VHF radio transmitting ground station that projects straight line courses (radials) from the station in all directions. The radials projected from the station are referenced to magnetic north. The radials are identified by numbers beginning with 001, which is one degree east of magnetic north, and progress in sequence through all the degrees of a circle until reaching 360 degrees. VOR stations transmit on a VHF frequency band of 108 to 117.95 megahertz.

Since the equipment is VHF, the signals transmitted are limited to line of sight to the approaching aircraft. Therefore, its range depends on the altitude of the receiving equipment. Generally, the reception range of the signals at an altitude of 1,000 feet above ground level is about 40 to 45 miles. This distance increases with increase in altitude. VOR stations are identified by its Morse code or by a recorded voice ID which states the name of the station followed by the word VOR.

The two of them had flown on an old DC-3 aircraft to Whitehorse, and from there, drove in a rented truck along the Alaska Highway to the turn off to Aishihik road that runs along the lake; some 135 km of dirt road that ends at the airport located near Aishihik village at the north end of the lake. The airport had been built for the military during WW II, but was now run by the Department of Transport. Aishihik village was a Champagne and Aishihik First Nations settlement. The lake is named in the Southern Tuchone Indian language, meaning *under the tail,* referring to the shape of the bay at the north end of the lake.

It was our lieutenant's first encounter with North American Indians. The DOT station had a small movie theatre where they showed movies every Saturday night, and there was no charge for native people. They usually arrived first and occupied the back seats along the walls. The DOT staff had reserved seats in the middle of the room. The movie shown that week was a Western. And when the Indians scalped the white man, there were loud whistles and cheers from the natives along the wall, and our lieutenant in the middle of the dark room hung onto his scalp tightly with both hands, fearing a similar fate.

Lofty had been at this station many times before, and he knew the Indian chief very well, and the two were great friends. The next day, the chief took the two of them fishing in his canoe. Our lieutenant caught the biggest fish of his life, a lake trout that weighed in at thirty pounds. Aishihik Lake was a major settlement area for the Southern Tuchone people, and their subsistence needs were largely fulfilled through fishing on Aishihik Lake.

The four months had passed quickly, and in early September, they were back in the office in Edmonton. The whole of the office staff surrounded our lieutenant and wanted to hear what he learned from Lofty.

"Do you really want to hear it?" he asked them

"Yes," they answered in chorus.

"This goddamn thing isn't worth a cuntful of hot water," and before he could start on the next line, the women were fleeing the room.

So our lieutenant had successfully graduated from the English language and was now ready to start his first year in a Canadian University. He read *War and Peace* with a dictionary; he could swear and was much pleased with himself. Lectures in math, physics, and chemistry were somewhat of a repetition as he had already done first year in Hungary and was able to follow the lectures although he didn't understand every word that was said. He was surprised to find that English language course was not compulsory in the Engineering curriculum. In fact he was allowed to graduate without ever taking an English language course. Later in life, he has often thought this was a great shortcoming of the Engineering Faculty. The midterm exam was a disaster. By the time he had understood the questions, the time was up. This had made him study frantically; refraining from everything else, and the end-of-term exams he passed with Honors. He had not had much social life, but he was too shy for that anyway.

Summer was here again, and he was back at DOT. Lofty had retired, and he was assigned to another technician, who was much milder in his use of the English language. Their destination this time was the Yellowknife airport in the Northwest Territories on the north shore of Great Slave Lake. The town and surrounding area was home to the Yellowknife Dene First Nation. It was the largest city in the Northwest Territories supported largely by the gold mines in the area.

"What shall I bring you from Yellowknife?" he asked the girls in the office.

"Gold," they answered, and their eyes lit up.

But before they departed for Yellowknife, our lieutenant had a visitor. He wanted to talk to him in private. He was a man well dressed with a friendly disposition. He showed his ID. He was with RCMP Securities from Ottawa.

"Relax and let's have an informal discussion," he said.

"You were with the military in Hungary?"

"Yes, I was technical staff. I was a lieutenant with the air force in Taszar."

"What kind of aircraft were at the base?"

"MIG-15's: the flying coffins."

"Why are you saying that? Were they unreliable?"

"Yes, there were many fatal crashes."

"What we are interested in is the weaponry used to home on enemy aircraft. Can you describe it?"

"Yes, it was a gyroscopic instrument. The pilot essentially brought the enemy aircraft within a floating circle, and when the plane was within the circle he would fire."

"That is a very outdated technology," he said. He was obviously familiar with aircraft weapon systems.

"Yes, it is. That is why the Russians sold them to their satellite states."

"You seem to dislike the Russians."

"Yes, I do, and it goes beyond politics and the fact that they occupy my country. It is personal. They raped and killed the only girl I loved."

"I am sorry. Have you been trained in the Soviet Union to maintain the MIG-15 aircraft?"

"Yes, I was. I was there for six months in 1954."

"Can you tell us where that Russian base is located?"

"No. We were not told about the location. My judgment would be that it may be four hundred to five hundred kilometers east of Moscow along the Trans-Siberian rail line."

"Who was the commanding officer at this base?"

"I don't know his name. He was a spry old man well past sixty years. But he had a very attractive young wife. Is there anything else I can tell you?"

"Can you describe the troop morality at the Taszar base?"

"Well, we had been surrounded by a Russian tank brigade overnight and were disbanded. I really do not know what it is like there now. People have to go on living. Pilots love flying and they will go on flying. What would they do in case of a war? I suspect they would fly to Austria, the first chance they have."

"I thank you for your cooperation. I will keep in touch, should we have any further questions. In the meantime, enjoy Yellowknife."

He even knows where I am going. I guess the authorities do not trust me in Canada either, but here they are at least half decent about it, thought our lieutenant. *I wonder what else he knows about me.*

Unknown to him, his mail, to and from him, were intercepted by the RCMP. He learned about that on the second visit in the fall by the same security officer. He told him jokingly that that was the case and his secretary, a young girl of Hungarian descent, translated them for him.

"Your friend's dirty language caused us much embarrassment in the office," he said. "You have been cleared for now, and there will be no further visits from us. But we can not give you security clearance to work at stations that are part of the Distant Early Warning system."

In the fall when he returned from Yellowknife, he was flush with money. He had worked many hours of overtime and had no place to spend it. His friends, Paul and Miki, had worked the summer at the Banff School of Fine Arts, and they had money too. So on his return a big decision was made. Move in together to share expenses. His friends had made plans for those expenses already.

"We want to buy a sail boat and a car for the three of us." They made the decisions and he was always included to share in the expenses.

"The car is a 1950 Chevrolet and there is a fourteen-foot International Dingy for sale on Lake Wabamun. Your share is $500."

It was at the Banff School of Fine Arts that Miki met Ann. She was an English woman from Yorkshire and was traveling the world, working wherever she could. Ann worked as a maid at the school, Miki was a gardener and Paul was a dishwasher. On weekends they enjoyed the hot springs and trips to Lake Louise and Jasper and other tourist destinations in this beautiful mountainous paradise.

One day, Ann showed up in Edmonton at the new residence of the three friends, and it became a foursome. Ann shortly gave Miki an ultimatum:

"You marry me, or I am on my way to Chile."

Miki didn't want to see her get tangled up with Spaniards and bought her a ring, and they decided that the wedding will be in Banff over the Christmas Holidays, a combination Honeymoon and Skiing trip.

You have to be young to think up such a foolish combination. Miki wasn't exactly an Olympic skier, and for the next seven days with wobbly knees, he had been on his ass more often than not.

But they all survived it, and the foursome returned to Edmonton with great plans for the future.

Ann was a professional hairdresser, so she was going to work. And because she worked, she didn't have to do house work. It fell on the three men to do housework. And they took turns; one was the cook for a week, the other had to wash the dishes and the third was the laundry and vacuum boy. The roles were rotated weekly. And over the three years, they all learned to cook, that would have made some chefs envious. Some cheated when it was their turn to cook and cooked cabbage rolls, Hungarian style, that would last the whole week.

No ordinary married woman would fit into a three-man household like this. But Ann wasn't ordinary, she was special. She could love one man and make the other two her lifelong friends. They were actually very happy with their life during those three years. They had their routine. In the morning they put out two milk bottles on the porch with a five dollar bill inserted in one. The three men walked to the campus, and Ann took the bus to downtown to the hairdresser shop where she worked. They didn't carry keys; they never had to lock the house, nobody would want what they owned. When they came home, the milk was there with the appropriate change.

They had their automobile and their sailboat on Lake Wabamun. On weekends Miki and Paul raced their fourteen-foot International Dingy at the west end of the lake at Edmonton Yacht Club, and Ann watched them. They were experienced sailors; they had raced in Hungary starting when they were ten years old and won many cups. It was like living in paradise.

Our lieutenant was envious. He worked in the far north every summer, far away from all this pleasure. But he did own a share in the automobile and the sail boat.

The next three years rushed by far too quickly, and they were graduating. They could hardly believe it. Our lieutenant was especially proud of himself, graduating from engineering in an English-speaking country without ever taking an English course. *Only in Canada,* he thought. He did pay for this later in life, struggling writing research papers, project reports, and preparing presentations.

Ann was now expecting her first child, and they moved into their own rented house. Paul moved in with his mother, who had just arrived from Hungary, to join her only son. Our lieutenant was hired by Cominco in Trail, British Columbia; a lead and zinc refinery. Suddenly they were waking to adult responsibilities.

He had an employment letter in his pocket to start on the first of June, more than a month away. So he walked through the doors of Canadian Imperial Bank of Commerce, where he had an account in good standing all through his student years, to ask for a loan. The receptionist ushered him to an office where a prim, stern-looking woman with glasses sat behind the desk.

"How can I help?" she asked.

"I would like to apply for a loan," and he showed her the letter of employment.

"You don't have an employment record yet, do you?"

"No, I have just graduated. But I had worked the summers in the Yukon and the Northwest Territories with Department of Transport."

"Do you have any collateral?"
"What does that mean?"
"Do you own anything of value?"
"I own a share in a 1950 Chevrolet and a sail boat."
"I am sorry, but our rules are very strict on loans without collateral. Maybe you can come back in a year."

Our lieutenant was wondering what she didn't like about him; his looks, his clothes, his accent? She never smiled.

Across the street was the Bank of Montreal. He walked in.

"How can we help you?" A woman just stepping out of her office, asked him.

Here we go again, our lieutenant thought.

"I would like to apply for a loan."

"Come in," and she smiled.

He showed her his letter of employment and held his breath.

"How much money do you need?" she asked.

"I would like to borrow two thousand dollars."

She got out some papers and asked him to sign them on the bottom line.

"Do you have an account with us?" she asked.

"No."

"I will open up one for you and deposit the money there."

"I don't have any collateral," he said and looked at her sheepishly.

"I am sure you soon will. I wish you the best of luck in Trail."

Well, what a difference. She didn't even ask what the money was for. I guess she didn't mind my accent, he thought.

He was now very excited. The Volkswagen Beetle will cost $1700 and he will still have $300 left over.

He had two friends among his classmates he felt close to, they were both Germans; Anton and Peter. Peter was much older than the rest of the class. He had been a German prisoner of war in Lethbridge, Alberta, and he had been so well treated there that after his repatriation to Germany he immediately applied to immigrate to Canada. He was married and his wife worked while he studied. They had two small children already. It was at their house that he ate raw meat for the first time in his life, hamburger German style. This was before the Japanese sushi bars opened up across the country. Anton was his age, and he asked him if he would like to go on a tenting trip to California.

"I have money to buy a Volkswagen Beetle," he told him.

Anton thought that it was a great idea, and they took off one morning equipped with a tent and mats, a propane gas cooker and maps to explore the coastline of Oregon and California and maybe even cross over to Mexico. They had a whole month before they had to turn into adults and report for work. It was late April, and the weather was still cool for tenting, but they were too excited to mind.

They decided to drive through Calgary and Banff and Lake Louise to Trail in British Columbia and have a look at our lieutenant's work place and tent somewhere in northern Washington state the first night. The location of Trail on the shores of the Columbia River surrounded by beautiful mountains had impressed them, and now our lieutenant looked forward to living there. They still had maybe an hour of daylight, so they plodded on. But it was getting dark when they passed through Immigration on the Washington border and started frantically looking for a level spot somewhere just off the highway. The place had an open gate and there were no buildings that they could see. They put up their tent, and Anton looked around with a flash light. He came back alarmed.

"Do you know where we are?"

"No, where are we?"

"We are in a cemetery."

"Oh, my god, let's get the hell out of here."

They disassembled the tent in a hurry and drove off, back to the highway, looking for another level spot. They decided they will tent just off the highway. They found a level spot, put up their tent again and went to sleep. They were exhausted. They woke to a loud rumbling. *What is that?* They wondered, as the ground was shaking.

"I think it is an earthquake," Anton said. The rumbling and clattering got louder, and they realized it was a train passing by.

"The next time we are not going to wait till darkness to put up the tent," our lieutenant remarked.

Their next stop was the sand dunes on the Oregon coast, just south from Florence. The Oregon Dunes National Recreation Area extends for some forty miles along the Oregon coast from Florence in the North to Coos Bay in the South. It is a unique area of windswept sand that is the result of millions of years of wind, sand, and rain erosion. The dunes extend some 2.5 miles inland from the shore.

Putting up a tent in sand felt strange, but it was soft and clean. They felt like Bedouins living in the desert. But the wind blowing from the sea was cold, and the waves were splashing onto the shore in big waves. *Where does it get warm?* they were wondering. Tenting in April didn't seem so wonderful all of a sudden.

Oh well, California will be warm.

Highway 101 along the California coast line was treacherous, full of winding turns and oncoming huge trucks carrying massive loads of timber, and their little Beetle looked puny and vulnerable. For the two beginner drivers, this was a scary experience. It did get warmer south of Los Angeles along the Santa Anna coast. It was the first night that they were not freezing in the tent. But it still wasn't bathing suit and swimming weather. *Maybe we can swim in the ocean in Mexico,* they thought.

The next morning, they arrived at the Mexican side of the border, and they rolled down the window of the car and had their passports ready in their hands. But there was no one to be seen. *This is strange,* they thought. They waited a few minutes and then drove on. "I guess Mexico is open for tourist business" Anton said. And it was. They were soon surrounded by young kids, maybe ten or twelve years old. "Senor, I have beautiful sister, do you like?" The buildings were neglected, and the streets were full of scattered garbage and windswept papers. *What a difference from San Diego, just across the border,* they thought. *What makes the difference?* they wondered.

"Let's go back. I don't want to see this" said Anton and our lieutenant agreed. They never got their swimming suits wet in Mexico, but it wasn't warm enough for that there either.

Coming back at the U.S. side of the border they did want to see their passports.

"Where is the Mexican entry in your passport?" the officer asked.

"There was nobody to put it in there," they replied.

"Typical." That's all he said.

"When did you cross the border?" he asked.

"Maybe an hour ago . . ."

"Why did you come back so soon?"

"We don't really know. It just felt so different there, so poor."

"Do you have anything to declare?"

"No, we have enough money only for gas and food; in that order."

"Good grief, move on men!"

And they were back to California. Their trip only lasted two weeks and they were back in Edmonton. It felt so comfortable to sleep in real beds again.

When it was time to move to Trail, our lieutenant packed all he owned in the Beetle. It fitted in comfortably. The 1950 Chevrolet and the sailboat stayed with Paul. He had only a hundred dollars left and was wondering how he will survive to his first paycheck.

When he arrived in Trail the city was under water. The Columbia River burst its banks and flooded a large part of the city. It was the great flood of 1961. It was this flood that prompted the Columbia Treaty of 1961 between Canada and the United States and resulted in the construction of three large dams on the Canadian side of the Columbia: *the Duncan Dam in 1967, the Arrow Dam in 1968 and the Mica Dam in 1973* for purposes of flood control and power generation. The Cominco plant was higher up on a hill, and here he was greeted by Mr. Grey, the personnel manager who originally interviewed him at the University. Our lieutenant recalled how he had applied for work with everyone who came to the University and was turned down every time until Mr. Grey came along. And he didn't ask about his grades or work experience. He only wanted to know what activities he liked. He told him he liked swimming, gymnastics, sailing, and skiing. You are hired. And that was it. And here he was facing him again.

"Come along young man, I will show you to your residence. Engineers in training are housed in the staff housing. It is free of charge. They also serve meals there free of charge."

Wow, I must have arrived in paradise, he thought. *I can survive on my fifty dollars I came to the door with.*

Trail had a large Italian community, and most of them worked at the Cominco plant. They emigrated from southern Italy, and they were famous for their hospitality. They all grew grapes and made their own wine. It was here that our lieutenant learned that you don't visit two Italian families the same day. Not if you plan to find your way home on your own. The Italian wine they made was not only good, but it was potent.

Our lieutenant quickly integrated into the community. Very shortly after his arrival he was coaching the swimming team at the community pool that was built by Cominco. The two sons of Mr. Grey were in this group of young competitive swimmers. And some of the older sisters of the boys had their eyes on the young, sporty-looking coach. He was tanned by the California sun and looked Italian. To look Italian was almost a must in this community if you wanted to court a girl. But our coach wasn't ready for girls yet. You can't get serious with girls with just fifty dollars in your pocket.

The plant was a great benefactor for the community, but it was also a curse for the environment. The sulfur dioxide spewed out of the chimneys killed the trees along the Columbia River well along into the United States. The State of Washington sued the company and demanded financial compensation. The case set a precedent in international law that a country is responsible for the environmental damage it causes to another country. The company had to do something and the engineers had come up with a plan that was good for the environment and was also beneficial for Cominco. They recommended construction of new electrostatic chimneys that would capture the sulfur and turn it into fertilizer. The elephant brand fertilizer was born. But working in the lead and zinc refineries were still something else. Our lieutenant started to lose his appetite and didn't feel well. He had to wear a gas mask entering the plants. He also noticed that a lot of the senior staff died early and did not reach retirement age. This made advancement easy for new recruits, but it also worried our lieutenant. This was a great company; he would have had a great life, but did he want to die early?

He decided to seek new employment. He applied for a teaching job at the Southern Alberta Institute of Technology in Calgary and was accepted for the school year starting in September. Mr. Grey tried to talk him out of it; he hated to loose the coach of his kids.

"You should stay, try our winters. The Red Mountain ski hill in Rossland is the best in the country."

But our lieutenant had already accepted the position in the Calgary school.

This choice, however, did not turn out to be a good one. Yes, he had a University degree, he was intelligent, but he didn't really have any practical industrial experience that was useful to the school. So at the end of his one year probation the school released him and he was without a job. He decided to go back to Edmonton, where at least he had friends. Almost a third of his graduating class now worked for Alberta Government Telephones and they advised him to put in an application, which he did and waited anxiously for a reply.

"OK, while I wait I will have a holiday." He had savings, so he wasn't broke.

The sailboat was moored at the Edmonton Yacht Club on Lake Wabamun, and he drove out there. *Maybe finally, I can enjoy my one third share in this boat,* he thought. He didn't realize just how fatal the next two weeks will turn out for him.

CHAPTER 4

Fatal Attraction

Lake Wabamun lies sixty-five kilometers west of Edmonton, Alberta. It is a nineteen-kilometer-long and seven-kilometer-wide lake, with depths ranging from six to eleven meters. Its name derives from the *Cree* word for *mirror*. It has been the best *whitefish* lake in the Edmonton area and it is also well known for its *northern pike*. The shores around the lake are favorite cottage country for Edmonton residents. At the west end of the lake lays the Seba Beach community and the Edmonton Yacht Club. It is here that we find our lieutenant waxing the bottom of his partially owned International Dingy, preparing the boat for the scheduled weekend race. He didn't have a crew lined up yet, but he hoped someone would show up before the start of the race the next day. He was too absorbed in his work to notice the young woman watching him from the nearby cottage. The yacht club owned small cottages on its property and rented them out on a weekly basis during the summer to supplement the club's finances. She walked closer and looked at the boat with curiosity.

"Why do you have to wax it?" she asked.

He looked up and saw a very young woman. She wore glasses. She was very pretty with a slender build and there was a special light shining in her eyes that reflected gentility. *Irish eyes are smiling,* he thought.

"It reduces the water resistance on the hull. Are you Irish?" he asked her.

"My father was," she said, almost annoyed.

"Why, where is he now?"

"He doesn't live with us any more."

"Who are you with here?"

"I am staying in that cottage with my grandmother and my younger brother and sister," pointing to the nearest cottage.

"Well, you are not exactly grown up yourself."

"I had my nineteenth birthday yesterday," she announced almost defiantly.

"Happy birthday," he said relieved, but not quite sure why.

"Have you ever been in a sailboat," he asked her almost involuntarily.

"No."

"Would you like to?"

"I would love to."

"I don't have a crew for tomorrow. Would you like to sail in the race tomorrow? I could teach you the essentials on the shore today."

"OK." and she threw up her arms with joy.

"All right young lady, I have to teach you the essentials. I will bring out the sails, spread them out on the grass and show you how to rig the boat.

First we will have to turn the boat windward. Can you help me?"

They twisted the boat around on the sand with the bow facing north; the direction the wind was blowing from.

He brought out the sails and pulled them out from the sail bags.

"We have to unfold the sails. They have to be folded the same way when we are done to put them away.

We have three sails here: the mainsail, the jib and the spinnaker. We will not bother with the spinnaker. It is too difficult to handle the first time out. We will race tomorrow using only the mainsail and the jib.

We install these *battens* in the *leech* pockets of the mainsail. They help to maintain the smooth curved shape of the mainsail for best forward pull and least tilt. You may not understand these terms yet, but you will when you experience pull and heel on the water. Don't worry, I will not put you in any danger, we will go out and just enjoy the sailing. We will not try to win the race.

We slide the foot of the mainsail into this full length slot on the boom and tie it down on the end of the boom.

Next we slide the forward edge of the mainsail into the run-up slot on the mast, and pull it up with the mainsail halyard which we then tie down. The mainsail is now free to swing in the wind, and it won't tip the boat over.

Next we attach the jib to the bow of the boat and clip the shackles on the forestay and pull it up with the jib halyard, which we then tie down. The jib is now free to swing in the wind. During the race these two sheets on the end of the jib will be your responsibility: to trim the jib until the frontal edge of the jib stops luffing.

We could actually leave the boat rigged like this and walk away, provided the wind doesn't change on us.

Next we attach the rudder and the tiller on the stern. The skipper, which is me, will handle the tiller, the retrievable center board and the mainsail sheet. The crew, which is you, will handle the two jib sheets. When we tack, or jibe, I will give you the signal 'tack' or 'jibe' and you just let go of the leeward jib sheet, move to the other side of the boat and pull on the other (lazy) sheet and tighten until I say 'good.' You don't actually have to hold the leeward sheet. You can tie it down in the cleat on the ledge. During the tack or jibe you must keep your head down, so the boom doesn't hit your head.

That is all there is to it. Do you still want to do it?"

"Oh yes, I am very excited."

"For the best speed we have to keep the boat flat on the water. This is how that is done," and he stepped into the boat to demonstrate.

"We put our two feet under the straps on the center board housing and lean back."

"Wow, that looks difficult," she exclaimed.

"It is good for your tummy muscles," he laughed.

"Do you want to try it?" he asked her teasingly.

"OK, I will try, but catch me if I fall."

She stepped into the boat and sitting on the narrow ledge leaned back. He had his left arm stretched out kneeling in the sand. Her head came down level with his and his face involuntarily touched hers. She blushed but didn't seem to mind.

He lifted her out of the boat, and the warmth of her body against his bare chest stirred up a feeling from the past when Marika held him tight on the motorcycle.

She is the same age as Marika was then. But six long years had passed since, he thought and felt sad.

"Put on running shoes tomorrow and a windbreaker. I don't want you catch a cold. The start of the race is at one o'clock."

As she walked away he started pulling down the sails with a strange feeling in his heart. *I forgot to ask her name and if she can swim,* he thought.

He had a shower in the clubhouse and started walking up the hill toward the cabin. Miki and Ann, in the spring of that year, bought a half-acre lot up on the hill overlooking the lake for five hundred dollars and built a small wooden cabin on the property from lumber they purchased cheaply at a demolition site. It was a one-room garage-like construction with a small kitchen. It didn't have a bathroom; the yacht club had showers for its members. For more urgent things, Miki and Paul built a mighty fine outhouse. It had two major design faults; the seat was too comfortable and the half-height open door provided a magnificent view of the lake and people spent too much time admiring the lake view and reading magazines deposited in a box there.

This is where our lieutenant spent the night on a couch, thinking of the next day. *She is not exactly an ideal crew to balance the boat if the wind gets strong. Oh well, I promised her already.* Waxing the boat made him tired and he fell asleep quickly.

He was up early the next morning and made apple pancakes and coffee in a one cup espresso machine. He was now looking forward to spending the day with that mysterious nineteen-year-old woman. *Marika was young too and she meant everything to me. Can it happen again?* he wondered.

He was running down the winding path to the lake and walked the dirt road toward the club with a strange upbeat in his heart. It was early and he was the first to bring the sails to his boat. She came running from her cabin.

"You are early," she said.

She was dressed in a short skirt, a blouse and a windbreaker and brand-new runners.

"You might get those shoes wet. Maybe you should put on some older pair," he told her.

"It is OK. I don't have another pair," and she smiled with that sweet glint in her eyes.

"What's your name? I forgot to ask you yesterday."

"Diane McBride. What is yours?"

"My name is Geza Kalman, but my friends just call me Csipogo. It is a nickname. I think in English it means '*chirpy.*' I acquired it on account of my high pitched cheerful voice that forgot to change to bass at age sixteen."

"I love it. It has such a sweet connotation to it," and she laughed.

"Now that we know each other, let's get to work. But before we do that do I have to ask your mom or grandma for permission to take you out on the boat?"

"No! I am not a child anymore," and she shook her head defiantly. "My mother will be coming from Edmonton later in the afternoon and I will introduce you to her."

"Can you swim?"

"Oh yes. I am a good swimmer."

"OK, let's rig the boat then, and we can leave the sails flopping in the wind until the start of the race. It looks like we will have light winds today, which is good. This boat does well in light wind. Most of the other boats are *Y-Flyers* and they are faster than our dingy, but in light wind, we have a chance."

Because of the light wind the race committee shortened the course to just two legs, a beat and a run.

"On the second leg, it would be nice to have a spinnaker, but we will have to do without it. So I may have to rely on you to attach the spinnaker rod to the jib and then the mast when we tack around the buoy or we may just have to hold the jib out by hand. Here I show you how that's done."

The race started on time, and the *Y-Flyers* were quickly in the lead. Going around the buoy the dingy was dead last.

"Now we have to make a crucial decision, Diane. All the boats are running with their spinnakers up on the south side of the lake. I will take the north side just to humor them."

Halfway into the second leg, suddenly the wind changed and dropped altogether on the south side of the lake. The spinnakers on the *Y-Flyers* collapsed, while the north side still showed breeze on the water all the way to the finish line. And the wind was in favor of their dingy.

"If the wind stays like this we can sail across the finish line on a broad reach ahead of everybody. Diane we may just win this race. Lean out, let's keep the boat flat." Csipogo was beaming. He looked at Diane and admired how beautiful her slender body was in short skirt and fully stretched out.

And they won decidedly, with the next boat coming in a good ten minutes later.

Diane was ecstatic. "My first race and we won. I can't believe this."

On shore her mother was already waving. They ran the boat up on the sand. Diane jumped out; she clasped her mother's hand and brought her to the boat.

"This is Csipogo, and we won the race." Diane was beaming, her face was lit up with excitement and she was so beautiful.

"I am Mrs. McBride" and she extended her hand with a smile.

"My mother told me that Diane went out sailing with a man. I was worried a little bit, but now I am not. I am glad you took my daughter out."

Those were sweet words, he thought.

"Tomorrow we will have some barbecued chicken for supper if you would like to join us," Mrs. McBride said.

"I would love to," he said appreciatively.

The next day was Sunday and early in the morning Miki, Ann, and Paul arrived at the cottage.

"We will have a full house tonight," they announced cheerfully. "How did you do in the race yesterday?" they asked.

"You won't believe this, I sailed with a nineteen year old girl and we won the race. I took the north shore route on the run back to the finish line and the wind changed for a broad reach for us and the *Y-Flyers* were all stuck on the south side with no wind."

"That happens sometime on this lake. That was a cup race yesterday. You will get a cup." Paul announced.

"I have been invited for barbecue dinner tonight with her family."

"Good, that leaves more for us from Ann's chicken paprika" Miki said.

Ann pulled out a letter from her pocket. "This arrived at our house on Friday addressed to you. It is from Alberta Government Telephones."

He opened it eagerly; it was a confirmation of employment starting on the first of September as an engineer-in-training in the Radio Department with a salary of five hundred dollars a month.

"Wow, how lucky can one get, two wins in a row," he exclaimed with joy. "I will have to tell Diane."

"Who is Diane?"

"She is the girl I sailed with."

"Oh, it is that serious is it? And all three of them were looking at him inquisitively.

"I like her. She is a nice and gentle girl, and her mother is very friendly."

"That sounds dangerous," Paul said. "And remember, my mother wants you to move in with us. She doesn't like cooking for just two people."

"Don't worry. I don't plan to get married yet." He didn't realize just how wrong he was with that prediction.

During the week, he had looked at a waterfront cottage that was for sale for seven thousand dollars. But he didn't have employment yet, so he quickly wiped the thought off his mind. *But all of a sudden things look different now*, he thought. *I have two thousand dollars savings and a salary. I can afford the seventy dollars per month mortgage payments.* It was racing through his mind. He brought up the idea to his friends.

"That is a great idea," Ann said. "We can store the boat in front of our own place . . . I mean your place."

And once an idea germinates, it doesn't easily leave the mind. During the barbecue, he mentioned it to Diane and her mother. Diane was nonchalant, but her mother was enthusiastic.

"It sounds cheap" she said. "Where is it?"

"Not far. It is walking distance from the yacht club."

"Let's go and have a look at it." Diane didn't look enthusiastic, but her mother was excited.

The cottage was some six hundred yards from the yacht club. There was a small creek flowing on the right hand side of the building, and fish were fighting their way up against the fast-flowing shallow water. It was a decent-size cottage with three separate bedrooms with doors opening to an outside veranda and a large living room with kitchen and bathroom and a fire place.

"It just needs a paint job and it will look great," Diane said and suddenly looked more enthusiastic.

And the next week, Csipogo was a proud owner of a cottage and a five thousand dollar mortgage. *Now I own something of value, if any banker asks me again*, he thought.

When he got the keys to the cabin, it was Diane he asked to go with him to look at it from the inside. The living room window looked out toward the lake. It was a large picture window and you could see the pier and the boats on the water at the yacht club.

"It will be a perfect place to watch the races from your own living room," he said almost involuntarily.

"It is not my place," Diane said blushing.

"It can be, if you want," and walking up to her he took her face in his hands and kissed her. She kissed him back. They made love, and he suddenly realized just how much he missed a woman in his life both physically and emotionally. It had been six long years.

"I would like to give you an engagement ring, so your Mom doesn't feel you are in danger and fooled with."

She clasped his hands in her hands and looked in his eyes with that look, he so admired in her.

"I think I could love you, but let's wait a little while. You don't really know me and I am still in school. I had just finished my first year in the university. My mother wants me to be an elementary school teacher, like her. I would prefer to be a lawyer, a doctor or writer, anything but a teacher. I don't really like children. They frighten me. I think my mother just wants me to be married and taken off her hands."

"You can be anything you want to be and I promise I will take good care of you." He was trying to reassure her with sincerity.

"I know you would. It is more me I am afraid of. My mother likes you very much, I know that. She liked you the moment she met you. I think she wishes she met a man like you instead of our despicable father."

It was in April the next year, at the end of the school year that Csipogo gave Diane the ring, and Miki and Ann organized an engagement party in their house. It was the first time they danced together and his body fused into one with hers was a touching scene to behold. Those in the room felt a tinge of envy. But Csipogo, trembling in his whole being, was deeply oblivious to everything around him.

Diane's mother wanted a May wedding, and she quickly went to work on the design of Diane's wedding dress. Diane looked magnificent in it. It was pure white with the hipline taken in tight that made her slimmer, and the high-heeled shoes made her taller. She suddenly looked a woman beyond her nineteen years, and she turned even the Anglican priest's eyes.

Her mother's eyes were full of tears, and her teacher friend was tugging at her elbow. "Stay out of their lives," she was advising her. "He is mature and in love with Diane, and they will be just fine."

And for the next four years Csipogo was the happiest man on the planet. They moved into a one-bedroom apartment in a high rise building near the CN tower where Alberta Government Telephones leased several floors. It was walking distance to work for him, and Diane could drive the Beetle to University. The ground floor had a ladies hair dressing shop, and Diane didn't have far to go to maintain her attractive looks.

Csipogo's first major project was the new microwave route to Ft.McMurray, a northern city that was fast growing with the oil sands development. It took him away from home often, sometime for stretches of several weeks. When he was home, he cooked their meals to give Diane more time to study. Paul's mother was a fantastic cook, and she gave lessons to both of them in the art of Hungarian cooking and baking. They spent the summers at the lake sailing and fishing and entertaining. Their cottage was a favorite gathering place for their friends, and it reverberated with mixed English and Hungarian conversations and laughter. They graduated from the dingy to Flying Dutchman sail boats. There were two of them hoisted in births in front of the cottage. They owned one and Paul and Miki owned the other. The club had the largest fleet of Flying Dutchman in Alberta, some fifteen boats. Each year they took part in the Kelowna regatta and the Provincial Flying Dutchman competition organized by the Kitsilano Yacht Club in Vancouver. Diane developed into a great crew and enjoyed what it did to her body, and she did well in her school work. In the winters they went skiing in Banff with Ann, Miki, and Paul and reminisced about the beautiful life they had as maid, gardener, and dishwasher at the Banff School of Fine Arts.

Diane's mother was a talented piano player, and Leslie, a Hungarian doctor friend of theirs, was a great cellist, and Peter, the oculist, a great accordion player. With their numerous Hungarian friends, they spent many winter nights singing gay Hungarian songs with full orchestral accompaniment. The Hungarian church organized monthly dinner dances, and volunteers killed a pig and served freshly prepared pork dishes in old-country style to bring back taste and memories of long ago.

The four years seemed to pass far too quickly, and Diane graduated with honors. Upon graduation, a position was waiting for her at her mother's school. When she got her first paycheck, she came home waving it excitedly and glowing with pride.

"Now we are a two-paycheck family and maybe we could afford to buy a home of our own in the city and keep the cabin too at the lake," Csipogo announced. He didn't notice Diane's unenthusiastic response. The next day he left for two weeks fieldwork. Fieldwork meant overtime and savings toward their home.

When he returned, Dine was not home, but there was an envelope on the kitchen table. He opened it and started reading:

Dear Csipogo,

I hope you can forgive me. What is happening is entirely my fault, and it has nothing to do with you. You were wonderful. There is something in my background that you don't know and it makes it impossible for me to be the kind of wife and mother you want me to be. I hope that someday I will be able to tell you about it. I don't like children. They frighten me. I would not be able to give you the family you want so much. And there is someone else in my life and I am truly sorry. I know my mother will hate me for this.

Diane

His hands were trembling, and he felt like he had just been struck by lightening. *What am I to do?* he wondered. *You can't force someone to live with you, if they don't want to. You can't fight the other person either. The choice was made by her.*

He had a sleepless night. The next day he walked to the office and entered his supervisor's cubicle. Don McKay was sitting behind his desk, and looking up, he could see that his charge was very disturbed, and he suspected what it was. The previous day someone mentioned it to him that he had seen Diane at the theatre; clutching the hand of another man, who looked very much like the young lad in the hairdressing salon.

"Don, my wife left me, and I don't feel like working, and I am resigning my position. I don't know what I will do. I just want to get away from here," and he burst into tears.

"I know how you feel. When you have calmed down, come back, and we can talk about it. I don't accept your resignation. Take a holiday and stay away as long as it takes to regain your senses."

"Thanks, Don."

Csipogo turned and left the office. In the apartment, he threw a few articles in a small suitcase and got in his Beetle. He started driving south toward Calgary. Once on the highway, he pushed the pedal to the floor, and the engine in the back was screaming at a high pitch. Luckily it was a four-lane highway and no police patrol spotted him. At this point, he didn't care about danger. He got to Calgary in record time, in less than three hours. He regained some sense driving through the city toward Banff. The highway to Banff was a two-lane highway and was far more dangerous to drive recklessly. He drove through Banff and Lake Louise and turned south toward Radium Hot Springs. Coming through the narrow canyon, a vista of the hot springs opened up. The pool was full of bathers, and he didn't want to be alone. He decided to stay and turned in to one of the many motels surrounding the hot spring. He was exhausted and fell into a deep but restless sleep. He spent the next seven days here, lounging in the hot pool and swimming lengths in the cooler pool.

53

He looked up to the sunny sky each day and felt his mother's gaze upon him, and her voice echoed in his ears: "What will happen to you now . . . ?"

Slowly he regained his energy and started emerging from his depression. He decided to return to Edmonton and start his life anew again. His boss was happy to see him back.

It was June and the long Edmonton winter was finally over, and the sun felt warm. His friend Paul was a full-fledged school teacher now with the Catholic School Board and was looking forward to his two months of summer vacation. He knew his friend Csipogo needed a break away from his surrounding, and he came up with a plan.

"Csipogo, let's go to Europe and sail the Adriatic. My uncle works in a factory in Hungary that builds keelboats, and he can arrange a special deal for us. Two thousand dollars for a seven-meter all-wood construction sea-worthy boat delivered to Pula in Italy. What do you say?"

"I don't have two months vacation time like you do, Paul" was all Csipogo could say.

"Try, who knows, they may let you go." Paul was insisting.

The next day he mentioned his friend's plan to Don McKay, and his answer surprised him.

"It is not the usual policy of the Company to grant long leave of absences, but in your circumstances, I may be able to get you two months leave of absence without pay."

And he did. And the two friends were on their way to sail the blue Adriatic. Csipogo sold the cabin and regained his two $2,000 down payment to finance the trip. Looking back at it thirty years later, when the cabin sold for $250,000, he realized this was a foolish financial transaction, but at the time it seemed like the sensible thing to do.

Paul's uncle in Hungary got the boat ready, a seven-meter cruising boat called the Magyar 7. It is a very stable double-keeled boat with a watertight cabin and a self-bailing cockpit and it was outfitted with all the necessities to meet the challenge of heavy winds. Paul flew ahead to test it on Lake Balaton, Hungary's largest lake, and in sixty kilometers per hour winds proved it to be seaworthy. The boat was then crated and transported via rail to Pula, Yugoslavia, from where they planned to start their trip. They were experienced sailors, having raced in many regattas on Lake Wabamun, in Kelowna on Lake Okanagen and English Bay in Vancouver, but they were totally inexperienced in open-ocean sailing.

They proudly raised the Canadian flag on the stern and sailed out from the Harbour of the Pula Yacht Club on July 17, 1967. Their goal was to reach Rovinj by night fall.

The Yugoslav coast is a rocky, mountainous coastline, and the water is crystal clear. No green algae can grow to give it green color, there is no sand to make it gray, and here the water is truly blue. The water is transparent, and the rocks can be seen thirty feet down. It is amazingly clean. The water temperature is seventy-six to seventy-eight degrees Fahrenheit during the summer months. There are hundreds of islands along the full length of the coastline to make it varied and interesting. The first of these islands, a short distance north of Pula, are the Brioni Islands. These islands were designated as a military base and were on prohibitive list. Therefore, they steered far to the west to keep clear of them.

The wind became light in the early afternoon, and they soon realized they will be spending their first night at sea. Rovinj was still far to the north and they could not moor anywhere along the Brioni Islands. Tito, the president of Yugoslav Republic, had his summer residence on this island.

"At night we will be able to see the Rovinj light tower and navigate by it," Paul said. They soon discovered a strong light and sailed toward it. Their compass indicated that the direction to the light was ten to fifteen degrees west of Rovinj, but they assumed that to be an error in their compass. Soon they learned to trust their compass. When they reached the light at about four o'clock in the morning, it turned out to be a fishing boat with a powerful search light. The fishermen here use a strong light, which they shine on the water surface to attract the fish.

They were now ten miles west of the shoreline and Rovinj, but at least safe and far off the islands and rocky reefs. They arrived in Rovinj at nine o'clock in the morning, sleepy and exhausted. They moored in the harbor and went to sleep for the rest of the day and night.

Rovinj is an enchanting, very romantic place. It is a city which is on the mainland, but the harbor is surrounded by four or five small islands covered with green trees and flowers. The harbor is well hidden among the trees. Ferry boats leave every ten minutes and carry passengers between the islands and the mainland. Each island has its open-air dance garden with music every night. Dubrovnik and Split are better known places on the Yugoslavian coastline, but no one should miss romantic Rovinj.

They spent two days in Rovinj and then continued their journey north toward Trieste, the first Italian city bordering Yugoslavia. A chain of islands twenty miles north of Rovinj are officially declared nudist colonies. Since they were passing by anyway, they decided to have a look. They only had one pair of binoculars on board; Csipogo wanted them because they were his, and Paul wanted them because he was the ship's captain.

But soon the wind gained strength and they had to turn their attention to their vessel. With twenty miles per hour wind they soon reached Umago before sunset. It was one of those rare good sailing days. The next day they reached Trieste. Trieste is a real gem, a beautiful place. The city is built on a green gently sloping hill overlooking the blue Adriatic. It has no less than a hundred outdoor cafes, and these cafes are full of people every night. *It is a mystery just who looks after the numerous children in Italy after eight o'clock in the evening.*

The Italian coastline is very different from the Yugoslav coastline. Here only a few miles south of Trieste, the land becomes flat and the shoreline is a never ending expanse of sandy beaches. From Trieste to Rimini, a stretch of approximately two hundred miles is a constant line of hotels and umbrellas of bright colors. The effect of this is stunning.

The harbors are different here to; they have narrow entrances and sailing in without an engine requires great skill. The Italian spectators were impressed by the maneuver as Paul dropped the mainsail with great timing and Csipogo hanging out of the boat in the bow slipped a rope through the small eye of the buoy: they always rewarded the crew of two with loud cheering and clapping. The beaches are a great mass of people in the morning and late afternoon, but they become empty between the hours of 12:00 noon to 4:00 PM. The Italians have their afternoon siesta. But then at night, they do not retire before midnight.

They reached Venice in two days. Venice is a city of canals, bridges, gondolas, beautiful music, and great art. St. Mark's square is so huge that five string orchestras can play here without interfering with one another. Italy is a wonderful place for firsthand experience with history of more than two thousand years and art works of great beauty: works by Tintoretto, Tiziano, Veronese, Tieppolo, Caravaggio, Rafael, Bernini, Canova, Michelangelo. Venice, Florence and Rome are the three musts when visiting Italy.

The first great summer storm (Sirocco) descended on the Adriatic from the south on the second night of their stay in Venice. Winds were screaming at seventy kilometers per hour, and they were grateful to be in the safety of the harbor. But a week later, a similar storm caught them out at sea just southeast of the delta of the Po River. In the next one hour, they learned why so many churches were built by sailors all along the sea. The waves quickly built up to six feet in height. They had their mainsail reefed in and the storm jib heeled almost down to the water line. The warm salt water splashed from the bow across the boat and into their faces. They had to work windward to keep the sails off the water surface and were moving farther and farther out to sea. They were afraid that at this speed they will soon reach the coast line of Albania, a fierce communist state. Luckily the storm was over in an hour, and they could turn around and head back to Italian waters.

The Adriatic coastline is visited mainly by German and French tourists, and it is cheaper than the Italian and French Riviera, visited mainly by English and American tourists. Rimini becomes a German city during the summer. It has authentic Bavarian beer gardens and the gay beer songs and lively rhythm of music can be heard everywhere. After Cattolica, the coastline becomes rocky and mountainous. The cluster of hotels becomes thinner, and soon only small fishing villages dot the shoreline. Sardines, fresh bread, and peaches can be had cheaper here. Soon they reached Bari and decided to rest there before undertaking their greatest daring, to cross the bay of Taranto.

Once they got around the heel of Italy it was day-and-night sailing across the bay of Taranto, and they took turns at the tiller. The millions of stars lit up the night sky, and lights from the shore were reassuring. Csipogo was at the tiller when suddenly a huge water spout shot up in the air in front of the boat. He screamed for Paul to wake up, expecting some disaster.

"I think it is a whale, just keep your course" he said and went back to sleep; so much for bravado in action from a man of military background.

In the early morning, as the sun was rising on the horizon, fishing trawlers were on their way back to their harbors with their catch, and they were on a near-collision course with one of them.

"Hold your course," Paul commanded Csipogo. "We are a sailboat on starboard and we have the right-of-way."

Our military man at the helm didn't have nerves of steel that his boat captain had, and he tacked despite the order. Military training does develop an intuition to recognize when a battle is lost and there is a need for change of tactics. They could now see that the tiller on the trawler was tied down, and the only crew visible was hanging out of the boat with his pants down. That intuition saved their boat from disaster.

FIND A PLACE TO CALL HOME

Once they got around the toe of Italy they headed to Messina, on the Island of Sicily, which was their final destination. Here they sold the boat for more than they bought it for, and they were now ready to return to Lake Wabamun for more relaxing and less dangerous sailing.

Csipogo missed his cottage, but his friends had the cabin up the hill, so they were not without a roof over their head, and they were members of a great yacht club.

Back at work Don McKay waved him to come to his office.

"I don't want you to write about your trip in the Alberta Calls. We can't grant two months leave of absence for everybody in the Corporation. I have good news for you. We had been approached by Bell Canada to provide staffing to design and launch the first Canadian satellite into space for voice and television transmission. Would you like to go to Montreal on loan to Trans Canada Telephone System for one year? It will be a great year to be there, with Montreal Exposition underway."

"Yes. How can I thank you for everything you have done for me?"

"I am sure we will be proud of you and won't regret sending you there," Don said, smiling. And Csipogo was on his way for a new start in the greatest French city on the planet, Montreal.

Edmonton Yacht Club, Seba Beach

The cottage on Lake Wabamun

Sailing the Adriatic 1967

CHAPTER 5

Montreal Expo 67

Montreal is the second largest primarily French-speaking city in the world after Paris. It is the largest city in Canada after Toronto and the largest city in the province of Quebec. It has the enviable designation as Canada's cultural capital and has constantly been rated as one of the world's most livable cities. It has the reputation as one of the world's great nightlife cities, with night clubs with live bands open into late-night hours and excellent public transportation system to get you safely home.

In September 1967, Expo 67 had been running in its fifth month, and it proved to be the most successful World's Fair ever undertaken, with over fifty million visitors and sixty-two nations participating. The fair originally was to be held in Moscow, but for various reasons, the Soviets decided to cancel and it was awarded to Canada in the fall of 1962. It was Jean Drapeau, the mayor of Montreal, who lobbied the Canadian government to get the fair and celebrate Canada's centenary with it.

The exposition was located on four hundred hectares of a man-made island in the St. Laurence River and comprised of six theme pavilions, four provincial pavilions, twenty-seven private industry and institutional pavilions and fifty-four hectares entertainment complex of theatres, bars and restaurants, and open-air stages scattered throughout the site. During the six months run of the exposition, about six hundred concerts were presented; the La Scala, Vienna State Opera, Bolshoi Theatre, Hamburg State Opera, Royal Swedish Opera made their North American debuts, and several chamber orchestras, choirs, folk dance groups, singers and open-air dance bands provided around the clock entertainment.

Today the islands in the St. Laurence River that hosted the world exhibition are mainly used as parkland and for recreational use, with only a few remaining structures from Expo 67 to show that the event was held there.

Csipogo arrived in the city after four days train ride, in the opposite direction to that he had traveled as a student refugee ten years earlier, in 1957. His first act was to walk the campus of the University of McGill in the shadow of *'Park du Mont Royal'* where the six hundred Hungarian students had their first Canadian meal served: the finest *'rare Alberta steak,'* which to the great consternation of the chefs, they had all brought back to be ruined to *'well done.'*

He secured a small one bedroom rental suite in a high rise building on *'Rue Sherbrook'* on the twelfth floor. He was unaware that just two floors above him, one of Canada's rising political stars had a suite. He met him the next morning in the lobby on his way to Bell Canada headquarters. He was talking with the porter and had a red carnation on the lapel of his jacket. He looked modest in his appearance with a hint of shyness. Csipogo greeted them with a *"good morning"* and they both smiled at him.

"You must be our new tenant, I have not seen you before," the porter addressed him.

"Yes, I just moved in yesterday. I am from Alberta."

"So what are you doing in Montreal?" the man with the red carnation asked him.

"I have been transferred from Alberta for one year to work on a satellite project with Trans Canada Telephone System," replied Csipogo.

The man with the red carnation now scrutinized him with more interest.

"That is a great project to be associated with. It is very important to Canada, to provide telecommunication services to our northern communities, where no services exist today. The project is actually being fiercely debated in Parliament just as we speak."

"What is your name?" he asked.

"My name is Geza Kalman. I am an engineer with Alberta Government Telephones."

"My name is Pierre Trudeau, and I wish you success with your project. Maybe we can have a discussion about it again the next time I am in town."

"*I have heard this name somewhere before,*" Csipogo thought, and he wondered where.

He reported at Bell Canada headquarters and was escorted to a special section on the 10th floor that was reserved for the *Trans Canada Telephone System Satellite Group*. The majority of the staff was Bell Canada engineers. There were only three non-Bell staff; one from Nova Scotia, one from British Columbia and he himself from Alberta. Bell wanted to be the majority shareholder in this project within the framework of Trans Canada Telephone System.

The project for him turned out to be far more than just an education on engineering level. It was also an eye-opener to the realities of the commercial and political process and to the relationship of Quebec with the rest of Canada. Bell Canada strongly believed that they had sufficient influence in Government circles to secure the permit to construct and maintain the proposed satellite system as a commercial private enterprise under management by the Trans Canada Telephone System, in which Bell Canada had the majority voice. The carriers were acutely aware of the competition that a satellite system would present to their existing long distance communication systems should competition be introduced via a satellite system that is insensitive to distance. Their aim was to control the traffic that was to be introduced on the satellite system.

FIND A PLACE TO CALL HOME

The federal government of Canada looked on the project as essential to open up the remote northern areas of the country to development and pull it out of isolation and assert the country's claim of sovereignty over its northern territorial waters. They also wanted to prevent Quebec moving closer to France as the Quebec provincial government was planning to build an earth station to have access to the planned Francophone satellite network. And it was also imperative for Canada to secure the orbital parking spots from where to cover the entire country before others did. There was no disagreement on the need for the system, but there was strong disagreement between the various political parties about the structural make-up of the corporation.

The minority liberal government published a '*White Paper*' in which it laid out the basic principles for the '*Telesat Act*':

- The resulting corporation would be jointly owned by the Federal Government, the Common Carriers, and the general public through equity shares.
- The system would introduce television services in English and French to areas not previously served.
- The system would strengthen the links across the width of the country, but also far into the north. The reduced sense of isolation that this would achieve would have a strong influence in attracting personnel from the south to Government and industrial projects in remote areas.

Some members of the National Democratic Party (NDP) were especially vocal in their enthusiasm for development of the north and in their call for a crown corporation:

"Some members of this house will argue that there are very few people living in the north of Canada, that this is an expensive project and that it might not be wise to spend so much money just to please a few trappers and hunters, a few workers on the oil rigs, and a few Mounties. But it is important that we show some vision with regard to the possibilities of the north. It will not always be a wasteland with only a few people living there."

The conservatives argued that there was no need for government involvement at all, as the carriers were willing to finance, construct, and maintain the system, but they supported the liberal's proposal for a mixed private and government approach when the NDP tried to amend the Bill to turn '*Telesat*' into a crown corporation. It was interesting to note that all parties left out the native '*Inuit*' people from their arguments for the project.

But all this was just background noise for the engineers working on the project. They were assured by management that in the end the carriers will triumph and carry the project to completion as a private equity project without government involvement. So they diligently carried on with the design of the space station.

The city was still reverberating from French President de Gaulle's visit to Expo 67 in July when he uttered those inciting words to a large crowd from the balcony at Montreal's city hall "Vive le Quebec!" then added, "Vive le Quebec libre!" The Canadian media harshly criticized the statement. The Prime Minister of Canada, Lester B. Pearson stated that "Canadians do not need to be liberated." An NDP MP David Lewis was even more peevish saying "I am beginning to be very irritated by the way in which this mischievous old man of Paris seeks to add to our difficulties."

De Gaulle left Canada abruptly two days later without proceeding to Ottawa as scheduled. He never returned to Canada. It led to a significant diplomatic rift between the two countries. The event was seen as a watershed moment by the smoldering Quebec sovereignty movement and led to a rising tide of separatist sentiment in Quebec. And it fell on the man with the red carnation, Pierre Elliott Trudeau, three years later, to confront the radical revolutionary elements of the separatist movement by invoking the '*War Measures Act*' during the October crisis in 1970 as Prime Minister of Canada.

Csipogo thought, that being in a French environment, it would be wise to learn some French and asked around where in the city they might be offering evening classes in beginner's French. He was told to try Sir George William University. He had no idea just how far-reaching effect this choice will have on his life.

It was the last evening class session of the program and walking downstairs toward the front entrance he heard the pleasing sounds of Latin music rising from somewhere in the basement.

Why go home? It is still early into the night he thought. He took to the steps leading downstairs and walked toward the echoing sounds of the tango played. He loved ballroom dancing, and it raised an inner resonance and pleasure to hear the sounds of the conga drum, violin, and accordion and he started to walk with the rhythm of the music. He walked to the open double door and peered inside at the dancing young crowd. One couple especially attracted his eyes. It was such a beautiful sight to watch good dancers moving in step to the captivating and seductive rhythm of the tango.

"Can anyone enter?" Csipogo asked.

"Yes, you can, if you buy a ticket," said the young lady, with charming Italian features sitting behind a desk, and she laughed. Beside her stood a pleasant and confident-looking woman, with pretty oriental features in chit-chat with her, and moving her feet to the rhythm of the music. Not knowing anyone, he turned to her and asked if she would like to dance. Her face lit-up and she moved to his side.

I am so glad you asked me, I have been standing here so long but wanting desperately to be in there.

"What is your name?" she asked, looking at him cheerfully.

"My name is Geza Kalman. It may sound unusual to you."

"Yes it is very unusual. You look European."

"Yes, I am Hungarian. I arrived ten years ago to Montreal from Vienna after the Hungarian uprising. But now I live in Edmonton, Alberta. I have been transferred here for one year, to work on a project with Bell Canada."

"Are you working in the Bell tower? She asked.

"Yes, on the tenth floor."

"I had tried to get a job with Bell Canada, but they told me I have to be bilingual, English and French. I told them that I am trilingual: English, Spanish and Philippine. But that hasn't helped me. They told me that I need to learn French as well and possibly try again as they always need good people. So now I am just floating around. I had come originally just to see Expo 67 and visit my sister who is a nurse here, but I found this country so lovely that I applied for immigrant status."

"Yes, they are ticklish about the French language now. There are forces that are pushing hard to declare French as the primary language of business in the Province of Quebec. I had just finished my last night of class in beginner's French when I heard the music floating upstairs."

"I am glad it happened that way. Shall we dance?" and she walked through the door in floating rhythm with the music.

"And what is your name?" Csipogo asked her.

"I am Carolyn, but my friends call me Lyn."

"Will that make me your friend if I call you Lyn?"

"Yes, please do, and I will call you Csipogo."

Carolyn truly enjoyed dancing. She was light on her feet and danced with easy self-assurance.

"My sister and I plan to go to Expo 67 tomorrow. The Mariachis are playing at the Mexican pavilion. Would you like to come with us?" she asked.

"Yes, I am free on weekends. Where would I meet you?"

"My sister's apartment is on St. Catherine Street. If you take me home I will show it to you."

"Isn't it a marvelous coincidence, it is not far from where I live on Sherbrook Street?" Csipogo exclaimed.

"My sister will be off work tomorrow at one o'clock in the afternoon. We could be ready by three, and you will have two cheerful maidens to look after. We can take the Metro to Ile Sainte Helene station and tour the US pavilion and then take the minirail to Ile Notre Dame and visit the Soviet pavilion that I hear is very popular, and then wander over to the Mexican pavilion when we hear the Mariachis playing." Carolyn had her plan all laid out.

FIND A PLACE TO CALL HOME

They walked on St. Catherine Street arm in arm and they separated with pressing each others hands lightly. Csipogo walked in an elevated mood, skipping on the pavement in the late autumn evening toward his apartment, delightfully anticipating the weekend, knowing he will see her again. He enjoyed Spanish and Mexican music and he could almost hear the sounds of the castanets and the trumpets resonating in the fresh autumn air as if rising from the St. Lawrence River.

There was also a strange lingering feeling of alarm in Csipogo about starting a new relationship, after his four years of marriage to Diane. *Maybe be it is too soon*, he thought. Her presence was still strong in his heart and not easily dislodged or forgotten. The wound was still fresh. *Is it possible to completely discard four years of memories, ever?* he wondered.

When he rang the bell to the girl's apartment, a cheerful voice replied.

"Yes, we are ready, come up."

When he opened the door to the apartment the two women were standing in the middle of the room dressed in identical outfit: knee-height black Italian woolen skirt and white blouse.

"This is my sister, Betty" Carolyn introduced her. "We come from a family of seven girls, so *B* stands for second in ranking and *C* for third."

"Are you ready to chaperon two woman?" asked Betty.

"Two such elegant ladies, with pleasure," answered Csipogo and it brought a smile on the two faces.

The Metro was packed to capacity, and they were pressed tightly against each other in the sea of humanity. After being dislodged at Ile Sainte Helene station, they headed for the U.S. pavilion. This huge transparent geodesic '*bubble*' inside consisted of multilevel exhibit platforms, interconnected by escalators and walkways. Entertainment was provided in a three hundred seat theatre on the ground level. The platform that attracted the largest crowd of children and adults was the simulated lunar landscape with full scale lunar vehicles. Space exploration was also given prime time in the video presentations as well.

What a huge waste of money, spent on exploring an inhospitable revolving rock in space. We have enough deserts here on earth that could be turned into oasis just by building desalination plants and with imaginative use of irrigation. It would benefit such a large portion of humanity on planet earth, Csipogo thought.

Coming out of the U.S. pavilion, they stood in a long lineup to the minirail to take them to Ile Notre Dame. People were leaping in the air to have a better look at the man at the front of the lineup. It was Ed Sullivan the host of the *Ed Sullivan Show*.

"Maybe we can ask him to let us dance the tango on his show" Carolyn stated mischievously.

"We are good, but not that good. We are not Argentine" Csipogo teased her.

"People who are very good at something seem to have a natural inclination for it, an innate thing, as if they were born with it" continued Csipogo.

"This reminds me of a story my grandfather narrated to me once, when I was very young. One of Hungary's best loved natural story tellers was Jokai Mor, and at the height of his literary carrier, he received a literary dissertation from a graduate student, who asked him to critique his work. He returned the dissertation without opening it with a note that told the story of a simple peasant in his village that was famous for his natural skill for removing surface tumors causing blindness. And he did it with the simplest of tools: an old fashioned barber's knife. He had a very steady hand. His fame spread to the very best eye surgeons of Vienna and the College of Physicians invited him to Vienna to demonstrate his skill. He had arrived there in his peasant clothing and knee-height boots and was introduced to the gathered distinguished delegation. But before being asked to perform the operation on the volunteer patient present, the chief surgeon brought him in front of a large scale drawing detailing the complex structure of the eye. He looked at it in amazement and stated innocently that he never realized it was so complicated. When asked to go ahead with the operation he pulled out his barber's knife from his breeches, and amid loud consternation of his audience, approached the patient. But his hands were now shaking, and he looked helplessly at the stunned audience. So you see, if I would have read your dissertation, I would never again dare to write another novel. I wish you every success in your studies, Sincerely Yours, Jokai Mor."

"So what is your natural talent? Carolyn questioned him curiously.

"I don't know yet. I guess I took up engineering because it appeals to the logical minded, which I think I am."

"I just want to work, have something to do. I am not good at being idle," Carolyn said.

"I will talk to my boss at Trans Canada Telephone System. He is from Bell Canada, may be he can give us some leads," Csipogo told her.

"Would you do that?" and her eyes lit up with excitement.

They got off at the end of the minirail at Ile Notre Dame and walked toward the Soviet pavilion with the massive hammer-and-sickle stone carving in front of the silver gray pavilion, which had the dates 1917-1967 over the main entrance to mark the fifty years of the U.S.S.R. It had a six hundred seat theatre, the largest at the exhibition that provided an ideal stage to politicize the great achievements of the communist system, the system that the rest of the world thought of as the '*evil empire.*'

"It is something that I will never understand about the human race: how can evil personalities like Hitler and Stalin rise to such power in supposedly civilized countries and bring about such massive destruction to the whole world. Even after having read the *Rise and fall of the Third Reich*, it still bewilders me," Csipogo said, shaking his head.

The Mexican pavilion was a striking white structure located at the waters' edge, complete with a Mayan temple made of ancient stones representing the Yucatan peninsula and the Mayan culture. The Mariachis were standing on the steps of the temple playing music that can't help but bring unbridled joy to the heart. A large crowd gathered around them and sang enthusiastically with the orchestra. It was hard to imagine that a thousand years earlier such temples witnessed the sacrifice of young virgin girls to appease some invented Gods.

The music put them in a joyous mood and they were leaving the exhibition grounds in lighter spirit.

"Don't forget about your promise to find me a job," Carolyn reminded Csipogo.

"It will be the first thing I will do Monday morning," Csipogo promised.

And it indeed was the first thing he did, and he was surprised by his supervisor's unexpected reaction.

"What a coincidence. Mr. Wilson, the head of Trans Canada Telephone System, just lost his secretary and he asked me if I knew a suitable woman for the job."

"Bring Carolyn in, and Mr. Wilson will interview her."

Mr. Wilson must have been greatly impressed by her, because she was accepted on the spot to the disappointment of many office girls with seniority who hoped to be promoted to the vacated position.

"Csipogo I don't know how to thank you. I am so happy," Carolyn beamed.

"I didn't do anything. You did it. You obviously have the personality for the job. Mr. Wilson is known to be very demanding."

Csipogo became known in the office as the boyfriend of Mr. Wilson's secretary. Carolyn quickly charmed all the other girls in the office and they became her friends. The young people of the office were soon christened the '*La Borgetel*' group. Their favorite hangout on Saturday evenings was the French bistro '*La Borgetel.*' The bistro had a great Latin band. When you entered the bistro you could cut the smoke with a knife, but in those days, the effect of second hand smoke on health was rarely discussed, if ever. After midnight the group moved to Csipogo's apartment. Carolyn loved to cook and served up delicious Philippine dishes and tropical fruits to the delight of everyone, and they sang and danced into the late hours to the great annoyance of the neighbors.

With the winter came the snow and Csipogo was eager to go skiing in the hills north of Montreal.

"But I don't know how to ski," Carolyn protested. "We don't have snow in the Philippines."

"You can learn. It is easy," Csipogo told her.

"I will try, but if I break my leg, you will have to carry me," she warned him.

"We will try Mont Gabriel first. It has gentler slopes than Mont Tremblant. We will rent boots and skies and poles."

But Csipogo overestimated his ability as a ski instructor. Even a gentle slope is a frightening experience to a girl from the Philippines. On their first run, Carolyn suffered bravely one fall after another.

"I think I have more bruises than I would care to show you," she stated emphatically. "I don't think this is a sport for me. I will have my gin and tonic in the lodge and watch you." And she became an enthusiastic *'gin and tonic girl*' in the lodges of Quebec ski resorts.

After the cold and snowy winters spring came as a welcome relief. They could walk the many paths in *'Park du Mont Royal'* and admire the city beneath their feet, the trees turning green, and the islands shimmering in the St. Laurence River in the distance. It was lovely to live in the center of this delightful city and have no need for an automobile. They had returned to the apartment, and Carolyn was preparing a light snack. It was May, and Csipogo felt the amorous call of the season. Carolyn had a summery dress on that showed the outline of her figure in the incoming sunshine. On an impulse he put his arms around her waist. She turned around and playfully slapped his face.

"It will cost you," she said.

"How much?" he asked.

"An arm and a leg and a ring." She laughed and kissed him gently.

"You have it" and he lifted all her five feet and two inches in the air.

They made love, and they were lost in the sublime feeling of two bodies in tight embrace all through the night. It was the first time that Carolyn stayed overnight at the apartment.

Just a month later in June, rumors started to circulate across the office. The Bell Headquarters will be split into Ontario and Quebec divisions. Trans Canada Telephone System will be moved to Ottawa to the new Bell Ontario headquarters building. The satellite group will be split off into an independent corporate entity '*Telesat*' and will be owned in partnership by the Canadian Government and the Telephone Companies. It all turned out to be true. The engineering staff working on the project was given a choice: join Telesat, or return to their companies. Csipogo and Edward the engineer from British Columbia chose to return to their respective companies. The Bell staff unanimously decided to join Telesat under very attractive terms of employment, carrying their years of service and pension benefits with Bell to the new company.

Carolyn received a notice of her scheduled move to Ottawa in September. That weekend they walked hand in hand and a bit sad in the park and deeply in thought.

"Let's go to Saint Joseph Oratory for a few minutes," Carolyn pleaded.

Csipogo did not belong to any particular church group; he gave up on religion a long time ago, when he was twelve years old. He resented being forced to attend religious services at the Protestant High School he attended in Hungary, where the sermons were preoccupied with life after death. He didn't believe in resurrection and life after death, or in a God that isn't finished with you even when you are dead. When you are dead you are dead, period. He could visualize hell, but not after death, but now here on earth, and it was not the creation of a God, but evil men, the war years taught him that. Religious teachings would have to go through a massive evolution to be acceptable to a reasoning mind, he felt. And such changes are not impossible as the Greek concept of Gods doesn't have much relevance today. He realized that Carolyn had a strong attachment to the teachings of the Catholic Church. The Catholic Church had a very strong influence in the Philippines.

"Without religion you have no spirituality, no hope of miracles," Carolyn told him.

"I believe it was the Dalai Lama, who said that there are two different kinds of spirituality," Csipogo argued.

"*One kind of spirituality is religious faith. But even more important is another level of spirituality that is spirituality without religious faith, which is simply to be a good human being, thoughtful, honest, and warmhearted. As far as religious spirituality is concerned, we can survive, we can live without it. We can even live happily without it. But without basic human goodness, humanity can't survive without that. Even if the individual can survive, that person would certainly be a very unhappy person. It is, therefore important that we teach our children from an early age secular ethics.*"

And these two people with their different kind of spirituality entered Saint Joseph Oratory that afternoon. The church was empty, and they walked up the center alley to the front seats. The renovation of the basilica had just been completed, and it had a seating capacity of 2,400. The Oratory's dome is the third largest in the world, and the church is the largest in Canada. The basilica is dedicated to Saint Joseph to whom Brother Andre credited all his reported miracles of healing people. Pope John Paul II beatified Brother Andre in 1982. His full-height statue stands under a sunlit side dome, surrounded by hundreds of lit candles, placed there by worshippers. More than two million visitors and pilgrims visit the Oratory every year.

Carolyn knelt and prayed with deep sincerity, which visibly lit up her face.

"So what miracle did you pray for?" Csipogo asked.

"I asked for a boy, and I told Brother Andre that I will name him Joseph after the Oratory and William after Sir George William university where I met you," she announced.

"Are you saying you are pregnant?" Csipogo looked at her inquisitively.

"Yes, I am."

"In that case I better get you that promised ring," Csipogo exclaimed, clasping her hand.

The next day Carolyn was proudly showing off her diamond ring in the office.

"To what extremes some girls would go, to avoid moving to Ottawa," her friends were teasing her.

CHAPTER 6

East Africa

The East African Community was established in 1967 and was a federation of three countries: Kenya, Uganda and Tanzania. The community designated four East African Corporations for common operation: The East African Railways Corporation, the East African Harbors Corporation, the East African Posts and Telecommunications Corporation, and the East African Airways Corporation.

Headquarters for the East African Post and Telecommunications Corporation (EAPTC) was located in Kampala, Uganda, and in April 1971, the Canadian International Development Agency seconded a team of Canadian engineers to EAPTC to help with the design, tendering, and installation of a long distance telephone network that would interconnect Kampala, Nairobi, Mombassa, Tanga, Dar es Salaam and Dodoma.

The East African Airlines DC-9 flight from Athens to Entebbe had Csipogo, his wife Carolyn and their two-and-a-half-year-old son Joseph on board to join this team of experts. The captain's British accent was reassuring when announcing the approach for landing to Entebbe airport.

"Fasten your seat belts. We are now on our final approach to Entebbe International Airport."

"Look Mom, they are fishing," Joseph exclaimed excitedly, looking out the window of the aircraft. Two African boys were knee-deep in the waters of Lake Victoria and were casting for tilapia. They were blissfully unaware that below the water surface *bilharzia parasites* were piercing their skin, moving from snails to human hosts in their development cycle. *Bilharzia* or *snail fever* is the second most devastating parasitic disease after *malaria* in Africa. People get infected when swimming or wading in shallow fresh water lakes and rivers that contain snails.

Entebbe was built on a large peninsula stretching well into Lake Victoria, and the Entebbe International Airport was located south of the city just off the water's edge. This airport, five years later on July 4, 1976, was the scene of one of the most daring counter-terrorism operations in history when soldiers from an elite unit of the Israeli army freed over one hundred Jewish hostages following a hijacking of an Air-France airplane by a group of Palestinian and German terrorists.

A Canadian colleague, Hal Lindbergh, was waiting for them at the airport. Once their few belongings were loaded in Hal's car, they departed hastily toward Kampala, Hal driving at one hundred miles per hour.

"Hal, why do we have to drive so fast? We have a small child on board," Carolyn cautioned him.

"We have to fly faster than the bullets. They are still shooting around here," Hal replied.

"Shooting at what?" Carolyn asked.

"Didn't they tell you? We had a military coup here. Idi Amin the chief of the military, ousted Obote while Obote was out of the country, and there are still some serious fights going on between the various military units."

"Why were we sent into this mess?" Csipogo asked, now visibly concerned.

"I guess, the East African Community still exists, and the East African Post and Telecommunications Corporation are operating, and Kampala is their Headquarters. We have not been given instructions to leave," Hal replied. "You will be staying at the Grand Hotel until a house is assigned to your family by EAPTC."

"Where is the hotel?" Carolyn asked.

"It is located in downtown Kampala. It is a luxury hotel. It has a gorgeous swimming pool, and it has a band playing nightly," Hal said, laughing.

"And outside they are shooting to liven up the cocktail hours,"

Csipogo chimed in.

"How long does it take to get a house?" Carolyn asked.

"We got ours in two weeks. It is a beautiful colonial home with an acre of garden and shamba for a gardener up on one of the hills. Nearly all the residents in the area are expatriates, mostly British nationals. Kampala is built on seven hills, like Rome. This really is a beautiful city with an unbelievable climate. The annual average temperature, because of the elevation (3,700 feet) and the lake effects from Lake Victoria, is twenty-one degrees Celsius, and it rains every day. It comes almost like clockwork. The clouds move in around three o'clock in the afternoon, and it rains for half an hour, and then the sun comes out and steam will start rising, and the smell of coffee and tea plantations and the multitude of wild orchids will fill the air," Hal explained, beaming with enthusiasm.

"Yes, I read about Lake Victoria, that it is huge. It is covering some twenty-seven thousand square miles with a shore line of three thousand miles. It has numerous rivers entering it, but 80 percent of its water comes from direct precipitation, and it has only one outlet at Jinja, which is the starting point of the White Nile," said Csipogo, trying to show off his knowledge.

"Yes, you got it. The White Nile is a fast-flowing, turbulent, rocky stream from Jinja to Murchison Falls, where it narrows to a 23 foot gorge and plunges 141 feet. Beyond that it changes to a slow and wide river, with crocodiles waiting on the shoreline for human victims coming through. And I heard there have been plenty of them coming through lately. Idi Amin's troops have done a good job of that. They weeded out the Langi and Acholi tribesmen in the army, as Idi Amin saw them as Obote sympathizers, and replaced them with men from his own Kakwa tribe. Tens of thousands of soldiers and political opponents were killed and dumped into the river," Hal said and shuddered.

"But the local Baganda people celebrated the downfall of Obote dancing in the streets of Kampala. It is being said that they never forgave Obote for ending the centuries old kingdom and sending the Kabaka, the king of the Baganda into exile," Hal continued.

They arrived at the hotel without incident and were checked in to a spacious room on the first floor, overlooking the swimming pool. The hotel itself was surrounded by an extensive flowering garden. Csipogo was excited; he loved swimming and doing it in a tropical paradise was an especially attractive prospect and he looked forward with anticipation to the next day. His son, Joseph, was excited too.

"Dad, you have to teach me how to swim."

"I will, I promise!"

And that was the first thing they did the next morning. Csipogo swam a few pool lengths and then let his three-year-old jump from the curb into his arms, and let him submerge just ever so slightly, to teach him to hold his breath. An African man of very powerful and large stature, who looked like a heavy-weight boxer, was sitting on the edge of the pool. He jumped in and swam close to them.

"Your son is very beautiful. He looks Eurasian."

"Yes, his mother is from the Philippines," Csipogo replied.

"Children of mixed racial background are usually very beautiful. We have beautiful people in Uganda too. People who come from mixed African and Arabic background or mixed African and East Indian background. Unfortunately East Indian woman don't like marrying African men. But I am going to change that," he said very emphatically, and Csipogo looked at him surprised.

He didn't realize who this man was and that he meant what he said. Only when a man dressed in uniform approached them and announced: "Your Excellency, your car is waiting," did he start to have an inkling, just who this man might be.

"Carolyn, I think I just met Idi Amin," he announced, returning to their room.

"Oh my god and what did he have to say?" She looked at him alarmed.

"He made some racial comments about East Indian woman, but he liked Joseph."

"Mommy, I peed in the swimming pool with Idi Amin," Joseph announced triumphantly.

"You didn't."

"Yes, I did," and he laughed.

"Hal told me that as part of the arrangement with the East African Community, we can buy a car duty-free and we will be given a diplomatic license plate. I saw a small Fiat car for eighteen thousand Ugandan schillings. Can we afford to buy that?" Carolyn asked Csipogo, blushing.

"Yes, we can, if that's what you want."

"Yes. I don't want to be stuck up on a hill without transportation."

And the next day they were the proud owners of a small Fiat car with a diplomatic license plate. Csipogo's adventurous wife with her three-year-old child on board had to try it out, despite all the dangers, and drove it to Hal's place to meet his wife Denise, and look at their home.

On their way back around noon, in broad daylight, Carolyn slowed down and stopped at the side of the road; Joseph wanted to pee. Suddenly she was facing a man in uniform with his gun aimed at her and demanding the keys to the car. This unfortunate would be robber didn't realize he was taking on a Philippine tigress with her cub. She quickly put the car in gear and drove it straight at the man with the gun, with the gas-pedal down to the floor. He had to throw the gun and jump in the ditch to avoid being run down. Carolyn was now driving at top speed through the city with the car horn blaring. She was desperate, as her would-be robbers were following her in their own vehicle. The cars of the oncoming traffic tooted their horns, not knowing what was going on. Only when she turned to the hotel, did the robbers pass by. Carolyn collapsed in a chair in the bar of the lobby and ordered a stiff drink. She was clutching her son tightly, and she was shaking. Dave and Florence, the other Canadian couple still at the hotel, tried hard to console her with their own drinks in hand.

This experience would have sent any ordinary woman back to Canada on the next flight, but Carolyn persevered and encouraged her husband even though Csipogo started to have second thoughts about the wisdom of undertaking this assignment. But he quickly settled in at the office, and they were now looking forward to the day when they could move in to their own home. And that didn't take long as one of the British expatriate's tour of duty was up after some twenty years of living in Uganda, and his furnished home was assigned to them upon his departure the following week. It had an acre of garden around it, and the resident gardener was happy to stay with his new employers.

The house was in the shadows of two huge trees, one avocado and one mango tree, and scattered across the garden lay clusters of banana trees both the edible and the cooking variety, decorating the landscape together with palm trees and flowering bougainvilleas along the fence. The house was very spacious colonial-style bungalow with tiled roof, a large living room with large windows and outdoor terrace overlooking the garden. The garden under Carolyn's direction and the gardener's diligent work produced everything they desired: potatoes, tomatoes, lettuce, cucumbers, cassava, yams, cabbage, kohlrabi, radishes, peas, beans and sweet corn. The fertile volcanic red soil and the year around warm climate with daily rainfall produced three consecutive crops of corn in the year. No humans should go hungry in this land or monkeys for that matter. The very first night they moved in, they woke to a loud clattering on the roof.

A troop of vervet monkeys were discarding the mango pits after having gorged themselves on the flesh of the sweet fruit.

Life was relatively peaceful in Uganda for the next sixteen months, and allowed the CIDA team to make good progress with the microwave radio project. After reviewing the radio path profiles, prepared previously by surveyors of the International Telecommunications Union, they selected the frequency plan to be used and established the required antenna heights and tower heights and prepared the tender documents for release to international bidding. A major decision was taken at this point to help the local economy and build the microwave towers locally. This was a unique approach never seen anywhere else. They decided to build concrete towers using local labor, instead of using steel towers. These towers also served as equipment buildings and housed the power and radio equipment as well. The towers were built by manual labor, section by section, as scaffolding was lifted higher and higher. After evaluation of tenders, the radio project was awarded to Fujitsu of Japan to furnish and install the equipment.

The relative peace in the country side also allowed traveling to Uganda's famous game parks in relative safety. Uganda's game parks are truly the best in Africa. Murchison Falls National Park was the first that the Canadian team visited, driving in convoy for safety. It is located 190 miles northwest from Kampala, and it is the largest of Uganda's game parks; it measures close to 1,340 square miles. It is home to all the large African wild animals including elephants, water buffalos, rhinos, lions, leopards, giraffes, hippos, crocodiles, wildebeest and a whole variety of water birds. The Paraa Safari Lodge has a large parking lot for visitors. They parked their vehicles and settled in at the lodge for the night. They had their dinner on the open-air terrace and from here they could keep an eye on the vehicles, that they were not broken in or worse stolen by thieves. They never in their wildest dreams would have predicted what was to follow. Suddenly a small heard of wild elephants emerged from the bush and ran through the parking lot, and one large female elephant decided to move between the parked cars and tossed them left and right like pop cans with her rump. They learned later that her name was Nelly, and that she had done this before. Doors on two vehicles were dented; otherwise the damage was relatively minor. Carolyn's Italian Fiat was spared. Nelly seemed to prefer the French '*Peugeots.*' These vehicles were the number one choice of thieves in Uganda as well. Buying luxury cars had certain disadvantages in Uganda.

The next day they started out early for a cruise on the river to Murchison Falls in a fairly large steel-bottom boat. They soon learned why the steel bottom was necessary as the numerous hippopotamus in the river started bumping their boat from below. All along the shore line of the now slow flowing White Nile, crocodiles were sunning themselves with their mouths wide open, and just twenty feet away, African men were casting their lines for Nile Perch. In these waters Nile Perch can grow to two hundred pounds, and landing them would not be easy with these huge crocodiles looking on. Small herds of elephants could also be seen roaming along the water's edge.

Joseph wanted to pee, so Carolyn lifted him up to do it over the railing. Csipogo got his camera out to photograph his son in the act with the picturesque background. Joseph was looking at the crocodiles with concern.

"Be careful, Joseph, the crocodiles might bite it off," his dad teased him.

The child didn't think it was funny and started to cry. But it was a much talked about picture.

The boat came very close to the bottom of the fall and the ferocity of the flow of water through the narrow gorge presented a spectacular view. Imagining that not so long ago, tens of thousands of human bodies came swirling through here made everyone in the boat shudder. Murchison Falls National Park would be a proper place to erect a plaque and remind people of the world of what atrocities men are capable of in the pursuit of power.

Queen Elizabeth National Park was the next destination for the group a month later. The park had been named after Queen

Elizabeth and was established in 1954. It is located 234 miles southwest of Kampala by road. It occupies approximately 764 square miles, an area that extends from Lake George in the northeast to Lake Edward in the southeast and includes the Kazinga channel that interconnects the two lakes. It is home to some ninety-five species of mammals and over five hundred species of birds. It is famous for its tree-climbing lions, whose males sport black manes, a feature unique to the lions in this area. It is also famous for its volcanic features and includes many crater lakes. The view is stunning as the winding mountainous road suddenly opens up to wide expanse of valley with thousands upon thousands of impalas and Thompson gazelles grazing as far as the eye can see.

Another month later, the Canadian group undertook a really ambitious trip to Kidepo Valley National Park in the far northeastern corner of Uganda, bordering the Sudan. It lies some 320 miles northeast from Kampala, and extends over 557 square miles of a rugged semidesert. It was established in 1960 under the first rule by Milton Obote, who forcibly evicted the Ik people out of the fertile Kidepo valley, a virtual oasis along the Kidepo River, which resulted in wide-spread famine for the local Ik people. A second disaster was perpetrated on the Ik people by Idi Amin, who ordered them to wear clothes. These people walked basically naked for centuries in harmony with the hot and dry climate of the region without much water to wash and keep clean. Wearing clothes resulted in outbreak of many diseases.

Moroto is the last major town in the area, some 140 miles south from the park. The group stopped in Moroto at a petrol station to fill up. Csipogo and Joseph went inside to buy some bottled drink. They emerged to a scene from biblical times. A group of men with sticks were chasing a man completely naked, who was screaming loudly. At the service station, he ran up to Carolyn's car asking for a ride, articulating something desperately. Carolyn quickly secured all the doors. It turned out he wanted a ride to the police station to escape from the menacing crowd. He was an Ik from the country side.

Csipogo reminded Carolyn of the incident many times afterward:

"You really blew it. You will never have a chance like that again in your lifetime: a man completely naked, well equipped, and asking for a ride."

The elephants in Kidepo Valley National Park are very different from other game parks. Fewer tourists venture this far north in Uganda, and the elephants here are more wild and threatening toward humans. Seeing several members of the herd flap their ears outward and run forward toward the cars on the road can be very frightening, and the Canadian group was undecided whether to move forward or move in reverse.

Then on August 4, 1972, all hell broke loose in Uganda. Rumor had it that Idi Amin asked an East Indian woman from a wealthy family to become his fourth wife, and he was rejected. Muslim religion allowed up to four wives for those who could afford to support them in separate households. He lashed out and ordered all East Indian people to leave the country within three months.

"Those who elect to stay will feel the fire of hell under their butts," he told them.

He accused them of hoarding money abroad and sabotaging the Ugandan economy. He confiscated their homes, shops, plantations, and manufacturing facilities, and distributed them among his cronies. It resulted in complete breakdown of the Ugandan economy. The new African owners had no experience in running these enterprises. Industry after industry collapsed: coffee plantations, tea plantations, sugar factories. Concrete production came to a halt, and with it the building industry collapsed. Uganda suddenly had no capable managers, traders, and builders. It wasn't until Museveni had become president in 1986 and asked the expelled East Indian population to return and help to rebuild the Ugandan economy and returned their properties that the country started to prosper again.

In August 1972 CIDA decided to remove the Canadian team from Kampala and relocate the project staff to Nairobi and Dar es

Salaam. Csipogo, Carolyn and Joseph crossed the Uganda border to Kenya in their Fiat without incident under the influence of their diplomatic license plate and were on their way to Dar es Salaam.

They spent their first night in a hotel in Eldoret in the western highlands. With the elevation of seven thousand feet, the nights were quite cool even though the place lies on the equator. It was astonishing to find fire places as a regular feature of homes here.

The next day they reached the Great Rift Valley that runs north and south and bisects the highlands to west and east highlands. The valley contains a number of alkaline lakes where lesser flamingoes thrive in the millions. They feed on the algae that are abundant in these lakes. One of these is Lake Nakuru. The Lake Nakuru National park is also home to the largest number of black and white rhinos in Kenya. At the gate to the park, a group of vervet monkeys surrounded the Fiat car. Joseph had a half-eaten banana in his hand, sticking out the open window. Suddenly one aggressive monkey jumped on the roof of the car and snatched the banana from Joseph's hand to the great consternation of the child.

"You are a thief," Joseph cried out bursting into tears.

"Well, he thought you were offering it to him," Carolyn tried to console the frightened child.

Crossing the Great Rift Valley, they saw herds of cattle guarded by tall, lanky Maasai men standing on one foot and leaning on a spear. The rift valley in southern Kenya and in northern Tanzania is Maasai country and they don't recognize national borders. According to Maasai traditional land agreement, no one should be denied access to natural resources such as water and land. Cattle and children are their most valued possessions.

Coming out of the Great Rift Valley, they decided to drive to Nanyuki instead of staying in Nairobi for the night, and stay at the famous Mt. Kenya Safari Club for a couple of days before heading south to Tanzania. The Mt. Kenya Safari Club and Wildlife Sanctuary were established in 1959 by William Holden, the famous American movie star. The combination resort and wildlife sanctuary straddle the equator and overlook Kenya's second highest mountain, Mt. Kenya. It has luxurious hotel accommodation, and small cottages and movie studios were also incorporated into the complex. White pelicans and colorful pheasants roam the manicured lawn and sun themselves around the heated outdoor pool. It is a daily show to watch the afternoon feeding of the pelicans. One particular pelican was always the first to get to the young African approaching with the pail of fish. She would rush to him and wrap her wings around him, and ensure she was the first fed.

After enjoying the Equatorial sun around the pool for a couple of days and more swimming lessons for Joseph, they were now ready to cross the border to Tanzania. Their Ugandan diplomatic license plate was valid in all three countries of the East African Community. Their new destination was Mount Meru Game Sanctuary, which is located on the slopes of Mt. Meru in the northern part of Tanzania: in the vicinity of Mt. Kilimanjaro. This Game Park and Sanctuary was established by Dr. Endre Nagy, a Hungarian immigrant who settled here in 1958. Csipogo was eager to meet another Hungarian in the middle of Africa who grew up in Keszthely, the city where the Festetics castle is located, and only a short distance from Taszar. In true Hungarian hospitality, he put them up in his home and took Joseph under his wings. He brought a three-week-old orphaned lion to the house and placed it in Joseph's arms so that he could hold it like a kitten. This scene has remained one of Joseph's most cherished memories from Africa.

Their next destination was the Ngorogongo Conservation Area. The Ngorongoro Crater, a large volcanic caldera lies within this area, 112 miles west of Arusha. The crater formed some two million years ago. It is two thousand feet deep and covers one hundred square miles. Estimates of the height of the original volcano range from fifteen thousand to nineteen thousand feet, which puts it in the company of Mt. Kilimanjaro. Aside from herds of zebras, wildebeests, and gazelles, the crater is home to the Big Five: rhinoceros, lion, leopard, elephant, and buffalo, with an estimated twenty-five thousand animals within the crater. It is a unique enclosed environment to observe these animals interacting in close quarters: gazelles and zebras keeping an eye on lions only one hundred feet away but unconcerned. They seem to sense when the lion pride is not in hunting mode. There was a young lion in the pride that limped around on three legs; it apparently lost one leg to hyenas. But the pride allowed it to share in the spoils of killed game.

The Ngorongoro area originally was part of the Serengeti National Park when it was created by the British in 1951. Maasai continued to live in the newly created park until 1959, when repeated conflicts with park authorities over land use led the British to evict them to the newly declared Ngorongoro Conservation Area. Land use in this conservation area has remained multiuse. It is unique in Tanzania as the only conservation area providing protection status for wildlife and also allowing human habitation. But land cultivation is allowed only on subsistence level.

Leaving the Ngorongoro crater they were now ready to start for Dar es Salaam, their new home. They intended to stop overnight in Arusha. Suddenly in front of them, a group of giraffes were crossing the road. Csipogo parked the car on the side of the road, and quickly got out his movie-camera to film the scene, and Carolyn was taking pictures with her camera. Carolyn was now five months pregnant with their second son and showed some bulge. Within five minutes, a truck load of soldiers stopped behind their Fiat. The soldiers jumped off with guns drawn and ordered them to the back of the truck. Someone drove their vehicle behind the truck. They were taken to a police station in Arusha, where they were interrogated about the nature of their photography. They seem to have accepted their explanation that they were simply taking pictures of the giraffes crossing the road. They were completely baffled why they were arrested in such frightening style. The military ordered the police to confiscate the film from both the movie camera and Carolyn's camera for further investigation, and they were released. Only years later, when dissident Ugandan troops with Tanzanian troops backing them, attacked Idi Amin's Uganda, did they realize what was behind their arrest. They were taking pictures in a prohibited military zone, and it was here that troops were training for this invasion. And their car had Uganda license plates.

After spending the night in Arusha, they were now eager to just get to Dar es Salaam and off the road and settle down in their new home. After reporting at the Regional Headquarters of EAPTC, they received their keys to their new home in Oyster Bay. It was a spacious, colonial-style home with red tiled roof, very much like the one they had in Kampala, except this one didn't have the mango and avocado trees overhanging the roof and vervet monkeys to disturb their sleep.

Oyster Bay was a rich residential area occupied largely by expatriates and embassies personnel in the northern part of the city, along the Indian Ocean, blessed with spectacular sandy beaches. The Dar es Salaam Yacht Club was located here in Msasani Bay, and for the next two years Csipogo had the best sailing experience of his life in these waters and winning many trophies, racing *Ospreys*. The club was located in a bay inside the coral reef, and it was generally accepted theory that sharks had never been spotted within the boundaries of the bay, inside the coral reef. That was the theory until one particular day, Csipogo and his Finish crew saw a hammerhead pass under their boat, just below the center board. From there on, whenever a boat capsized in strong winds, the crew scrambled to right the boat much quicker than it had been the practice in the past.

The regional EAPTC office had the responsibility to manage the construction of the microwave route from Mombassa south through Tanga and Dar es Salaam to Dodoma. Another team located in Nairobi was to manage the construction of the section from Mombassa west through Nairobi to Kampala. The section in Uganda presented the greatest challenge with the expulsion of the East Indian population from Uganda and the resultant lack of skills and construction materials.

In Tanzania, construction of a railway line was simultaneously underway with Chineese Government help to connect Dar es

Salaam with Zambia to bring copper shipments to the port of Dar es Salaam. Chinese railway workers by the thousands flooded the country side. They lived in their own compounds along the railway right-of-way and purchased raw materials for food. It inflated the prices for basic food items, and their exclusiveness created much resentment in the local population, as they contributed very little to the local economy.

Csipogo had two Tanzanian engineers, Kato and Kayani, seconded to him to help with the project, and a specially selected local group of technicians to maintain the system when turned up for operation, and the Canadian team left. Kato was born into a Moslem family, and his father had four wives. Kato had a twin brother and two sisters. He also had numerous half brothers and sisters who lived in separate households with their mothers. Kato himself met and married a Catholic girl at university and according to Christian tradition, could only have one wife. Csipogo used to tease him about that:

'Kato do you think you made a mistake marrying a Catholic girl?"

"Well, I must admit my father had a good life. Among four wives he could always find one in a good mood," Kato replied and laughed.

Transfer of technical know-how was part of the responsibility of the CIDA team, and it was done by directly involving the local staff in the installation and acceptance of the system. The very first step taken was to organize the logistics for transporting the equipment arriving at the port to a leased warehouse in Dar es Salaam and then dispatch them from here to the various microwave terminal and repeater sites in a timely fashion: antennas, waveguide, radio equipment, diesel generators, and batteries. To do this, they purchased two large four-wheel-drive trucks with automated lifting equipment in the back. By purchasing instead of renting, the Corporation saved more than the cost of these specialized vehicles and ensured the timely delivery of the equipment to the sites. These trucks turned out to be in great demand not just in Tanzania but later on in Kenya and Uganda as well. By the time the Nairobi team realized the need for these vehicles, it was too late to order them. Iliffe, an English man, was the leader of the Nairobi team and Csipogo remembered him as an eccentric and bossy personality. In his office behind his desk, he had a large painting hanging on the wall. It displayed a scene from Tsarist Russia where gendarmes were leading away a young man in chains, his mother and father in grief were standing in the background, and the caption said, '*the man who wanted to do things his way.*'

Carolyn was now seven months pregnant and decided to fly back with Joseph to Canada to give birth to her second child in Canada. She had a sister who was a nurse and resided in Montreal, and she wanted to be in her care. She didn't want her children later in life to have problems crossing the U.S.A. border and answer to silly questions from border guards:

"Where were you born, sir?"
"In Dar es Salaam."
"Where is that?"
"In the Harbor of Peace."
"Are you pulling my leg, sir?"
"No."
"Would you step out of the car and walk along this straight line!"

She just didn't want this to happen to her children.

Csipogo was left on his own for six months to survive on his cooking experience of years past when he lived with his friends during his university years in Edmonton. This freedom very nearly resulted in tragedy.

Csipogo, Kato and Kayani and Wolfgang, a Dutch born Canadian engineer from Nairobi, and Makena, his Kikuyu counterpart, decided to climb Mt. Kilimanjaro. It was a snap decision without any preparation for it. They started from a base camp in Maranga village at the foot of the mountain at an elevation of four thousand feet. They were going to climb along the regular tourist route on the south slope, on the Tanzanian side. Their first overnight stop was at hut no.1 (Mandera) at nine thousand feet. The mountain below this elevation had rich volcanic soil and had been under cultivation for thousands of years, and depended for water on the snows of Kilimanjaro. The fresh water streams are shared as a natural resource that belongs to everyone. From the main stream, they cut channels that are routed through each shamba. It is used for irrigation as required and then returned back to the main stream for the next shamba below to do the same.

The group was made up of five climbers and ten African guides, who carried on their head the beddings, food, and appliances. The five climbers were carrying only a walking stick, for which they realized the need only above the twelve thousand feet elevation. The second overnight stop was at hut no.2 (Horombo) at twelve thousand feet. Up to this point the climbers didn't experience any particular discomfort. Above twelve thousand feet, the terrain opened up to grassland, and the steep, snow-covered peak was now clearly visible. The novice climbers started to feel the effect of the altitude, and the group started to resemble the defeated army of Napoleon, walking very slowly, leaning on their walking sticks, and wondering if this whole thing was a good idea. They met a very loud Italian group, who were on their way down, who told them in no uncertain terms, that they would have been much better off somewhere on the beach north of Mombasa. They reached hut no.3 (Kibo) at sixteen thousand feet before nightfall. The night was freezing cold, and now they realized the need for the heavy sleeping bags, carried with much ease by the guides, who made this trek many times before. The hardest climb was still ahead, to climb the steep slope of Kibo peak to the volcanic caldera. This was planned for the early morning so that they could be off the mountain by ten o'clock as the noon equatorial sun would be too dangerous to be exposed to.

But no one was able to sleep at this elevation. Csipogo had a massive headache; he was vomiting, and his pulse was 160 sitting down. He just wanted to get off the mountain and gave up on the idea of reaching the peak. With the help of one of the guides, he made it down to the base camp in one single day. At base camp, he felt extreme craving for tomatoes. *There is probably something in tomatoes that helps with oxygenation of the blood*, he thought and gobbled them down one after another. He felt certain if he had carried on to the peak he would have died. The other members of the group all made it to the peak, but he never regretted not making it; he felt he made the right decision not to continue. There are many cases of novice climbers, who had underestimated the seriousness of this climb, and died attempting it.

Back in Dar es Salaam, driving along Ocean Road in Oyster Bay, he stopped by a vendor slicing fresh coconuts with a hatchet and purchased one. This had been their favorite stopover with Joseph to quench their thirst on coconut milk and eat the soft white flesh of the fruit. He decided to take a picture of the State House that was the official residence of President Julius Nyerere, something he had never done before. Within a very short time, he was surrounded by three uniformed military personnel and was asked to follow them. He was brought in through the garden gate to the front terrace of the building and was left there under the watchful eye of one soldier while the other two entered the building. He was told to sit down and wait. After about five minutes, two African men in dark safari outfits, walking slowly, came through the door in the company of the two soldiers. The two men waved the soldiers to leave and sat down opposite to him by the outdoor table. One had a heavy mop of dark hair and the other short cropped hair showing some graying lines. They didn't appear hostile to him and the man with the short cropped hair addressed him in English.

"You have a Ugandan diplomatic license plate. Who are you?"

"Well, to be honest, this license plate had caused me trouble before. My wife, my young son, and I had been arrested at gun point just outside Arusha a few months ago for taking photographs of giraffes that were crossing the road."

"Yes, my officers informed me about that and that you were taking pictures of this building," and they looked at him questioningly.

"I am one of the Canadian engineers assigned by the Canadian International Development Agency to the East African Post and Telecommunications to assist with the construction of the Kampala-Nairobi-Mombasa-Dar es Salaam-Dodoma microwave network. I have been transferred from Kampala to Dar es Salaam a couple of months ago. I didn't mean any harm. I just wanted to have a photo of the State House for future reference back home."

"Welcome to Tanzania, and we apologize for any inconvenience you may have been put to during your short stay with us. But we can not be careful enough. The dictatorial rule of Idi Amin in Uganda created a problem for all of us. This is my friend President Obote, the lawful past president of Uganda, and I am Mwali Julius Nyerere."

Wow, and he didn't even mention that he was the president of Tanzania. He is very modest, thought Our Csipogo.

"We are very appreciative of the help Canada gives us. Your country is one of the truly selfless donor countries that provide assistance without any pre-conditions attached to it. You can be very proud of your country. Tanzania accepts assistance from both the Western countries and the socialist countries, if the aim is to help the development of our independent nation. You can see that right here in Dar es Salaam with the Chinese building the railway to Zambia and the ITU with Canadian technical assistance building the East African Telecommunications Network. You seem to have an accent, where were you born?"

"I was born in Hungary and immigrated to Canada during the uprising in 1956."

"Well, isn't that interesting for more reasons than one. Dr. Endre Nagy is your compatriot and he is very much respected in Tanzania, for his work with preservation of African wildlife and presenting to the outside world the beauty of our country and opportunities for tourism and observation of wildlife in Tanzania. And you left behind a socialist country that was a failure, but then your country wasn't really free to develop their own brand of socialism. In traditional Africa, we are naturally a socialist society with our extended family structure. We just need to expand it to other aspects of life and ensure that it is a fair society and provide free heath care, education, and good drinking water to everyone. There is nothing more important for our people than being able to read and write and have access to clean water."

"Yes, I have just come from our attempted climb to the peak of Mt. Kilimanjaro and I have seen how that vital resource, water, is shared by all," said Csipogo.

"It is our aim with creation of the *Uyamaa* or communal living to extend that sharing to land and produce enough food for our people and free ourselves from imports," President Nyerere emphasized with great animation and led Csipogo to the gate.

"I wish you success, contentment, and happiness for the rest of your stay in Tanzania," and he shook the hands and smiled at his involuntary guest.

It is well known that the great experiment of *Uyamaa* didn't work out for Tanzania. Towards the end of Nyerere's presidency the *Uyamaa* owned 90 percent of the land and produced 5 percent of the countries food. The philosophy of sharing equally whether you contribute a lot or very little simply doesn't work. But his creation of a fair and peaceful society in Tanzania is a very important contribution to Africa, and Nyerere remained humble and true to himself throughout his presidency. "I am a schoolmaster by choice and politician by accident," he often said. And when, after 25 years of ruling Tanzania, he realized that he was no longer helping the country, he resigned and voluntarily handed the presidency to Ali Hassan Mwenyi. He ignored the trappings of power and remains the most honest leader Africa has ever produced. He truly believed in socialism and the equality of all human beings. To this day he is recognized as the father of the nation and was named *World Hero of Social Justice* by the president of the United Nations General Assembly.

After eight months in Canada, Carolyn returned with Joseph and six-months-old Gabriel in tow to Dar es Salaam. Csipogo narrated to her his experiences, climbing Mt. Kilimanjaro and his introduction to Julius Nyerere, and she shared her experiences of giving birth to a giant ten-pound baby, who was two weeks late. They decided to hire an ayah to help with household chores and with the children. The gardener introduced to them Florence, and they hired her. Florence was a chubby African woman, who was not sure of her birthday, who became very fond of Gabriel and carried him constantly around in her backpack, like he was her own baby. Gabriel was attached to his ayah very much and extended his arms to her every time she entered the room. He shared her meals on the shamba floor, eating like she did, with his hands. There developed a very strong bond between the child and his ayah. This bond expressed itself once in the living room when a wooden carving of an African woman fell off the mantle place and the child crawled to it, picked it up in his arms and cradled it, and tears appeared in his eyes.

Florence had just one tiny fault: she liked to drink. Every Friday night on her day off, she drank pombe. This is a potent African drink made from a variety of millet, and it is served in a large gourd. Men and women sit on chairs around this gourd with long straws and sip this beer like substance. New customers are waiting behind them until someone falls off their chair, and they take his or her place. Florence was always her normal self by noon Saturday and reported for work in a joyous mood.

It was June 1974 when the project had been completed and was turned up for operation. It was time to say good-bye to the staff. Kato and Kayani organized the farewell party and they presented Csipogo with an ivory carving, carved by a Tanzanian master carver. It occupies an important place in memory lane on the mantle place of their home. Gabriel was now one and a half year old, and his ayah was crying when she kissed him good-bye.

Their flight plan was Dar es Salaam-Nairobi-Zurich-Montreal, with a two week stop over in Zurich. During the flight, Gabriel became listless and lethargic. He developed high fever, and his eyes lost their shine. By the time they got to Zurich, Gabriel was very sick, and his parents very worried. From the airport, they took a taxi directly to the Zurich children's hospital. As a foreign national at the hospital, he was placed in direct care of the director of the hospital. Blood samples were sent to Geneva, and it took three days for the results to arrive. Gabriel had three varieties of malaria, both recurrent and nonrecurrent. It required special medication against each type of malaria parasite. It was a painful sight to watch this child, so young, suffer and cry in fright each day they visited him. It was always a tearful separation. Csipogo looked to the sky and pleaded, "You can't let him die, and you must not. He is your grandchild."

Two weeks later, when they were descending from the hospital, Carolyn turned to have a last look. Gabriel pulled her with both arms; he was not going to go back there. They were advised to continue with the medication for six months on the theory that the malaria will break out again, and the medication will kill it, and it won't be able to reestablish itself. The theory worked, as Gabriel never had a recurrence of malaria. The parents also made a vow: never again to expose the children to an environment of tropical diseases.

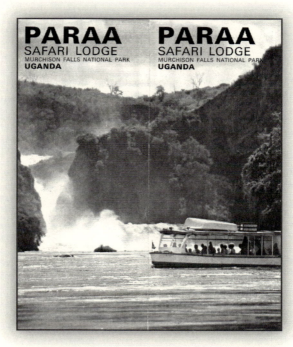

Nelly the elephant in Murchison Falls National Park

Elephant threathening in Kidepo National Park

Joseph with Florence and Victor in Kampala, Uganda (1972)

Vervet monkey attacking at Lake Nakuru, Kenya (1972)

Joseph with Dr. Endre Nagy and baby lion at Mt. Meru wildlife sanctuary

8 weeks old baby lion

Mtwara site in Tanzania under construction

The snows of Mt. Kilimanjaro

At 12,000 feet on Mt. Kilimanjaro

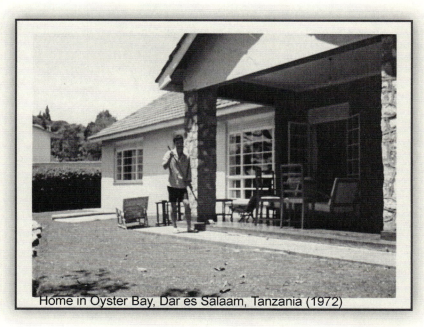

Home in Oyster Bay, Dar es Salaam, Tanzania (1972)

Oyster Bay, Dar es Salaam Tanzania Sept 1972

Sailing in Msasani Bay, Dar es Salaam

Gabriel with his aya in Dar es Salaam, Tanzania (1974)

Idi Amin

Julius Nyerere

CHAPTER 7

Saudi Arabia

It was in the summer of 1974 that His Royal Highness Prince Fahd Ibn Abdul Aziz, then prime minister of Saudi Arabia under King Khaled, arrived at the port of Marbella of Spain on his luxury yacht the *'Shaf-London,'* after breaking the bank of the casino of Monte Carlo. And this sleepy tourist mecca on the Costa del Sol would never be the same again. He declared it his summer residence and proceeded to build a royal palace fit for a king, a replica of the White House in marble and gold at an estimated cost of hundred million dollars, up on the hill overlooking the harbor.

It was here that Mr. Bechtel the president of Bechtel Corporation, the largest US engineering, management and construction company, met Prime Minister Fahd during a chance encounter in a downtown coffee house in Marbella. The prime minister instantly recognized the large-scale thinker in Mr. Bechtel and complained to him how he was distressed about the waste he observed while flying over the oil-fields in his country, seeing flared gas being burned everywhere. Mr. Bechtel agreed that it was indeed a waste of a valuable resource and that it could be harnessed and used as industrial feedstock in numerous petrochemical processes. The prime minister listened intently and asked Mr. Bechtel to submit a proposal. A master plan was submitted by Bechtel Corporation a year later, and it met the approval of King Khalid and the Saudi cabinet. A Royal Commission was set up under the direction of Price Fahd, and Bechtel Corporation was awarded the management of the largest industrial project the world had ever seen: 150 billion dollars over twenty years to design and construct Madinat Al-Jubail Al-Sinaiyah on the Arabian Gulf. And a new page was opening up in the history of Saudi Arabia, a page of industrialization.

The plan called for an industrial city that will be the site of some sixteen primary industries, chiefly petrochemical and metal producers, and a host of secondary and support facilities; all concentrated within an eighty-square-kilometer industrial area. Here the abundant petroleum resources of the region will serve as both fuel and feedstock in the creation of numerous products for use within the Kingdom and for export abroad.

Just north of the industrial area, a modern community for 350,000 people will be constructed along the shores of the Arabian Gulf. The community will be home to those associated with the new industrial facilities at Jubail, and with all the support activities generated by a thriving industrial and commercial center. Besides affording the material amenities that a modern city has to offer, the new community will provide a full range of educational, cultural, and recreational possibilities.

Supporting both the industrial complex and community will be such essential infrastructure elements as power and water systems, telecommunications networks, roads, railroads, seaports and an airport, and facilities for health care, education, public safety, and other social services required by over a third of a million people.

On the thirteenth of June 1982 King Khaled died and his half brother, Prince Fahd, became king. King Fahd had great affinity for the USA. He was reported to have said at one time: "We place our trust in Allah and after Allah in the United States."

It was on this day in the early morning that Csipogo received a phone call from Saudi Arabia from Dave Hansen, an engineering colleague who worked with him on the CIDA project in East Africa:

"Csipogo, I am now working in the Power and Telecommunications Department of Bechtel in Jubail, and we have an opening for an engineer. Would you like to come? We have a four-bedroom house just completed and fully furnished on standby for you if you decide to come. The salary is generous, and your kids can go to International School locally or anywhere in the world they choose, all expenses paid. Bechtel employees are considered guests of the king and are generously looked after. You will have to go through medical examination in San Francisco."

"Give me a second, Dave, let me ask Carolyn."

"Carolyn! Would you like to go to Saudi Arabia?"

"Are you nuts?"

"Just as I thought Dave, she said yes."

Csipogo learned that chance opportunities in life are not necessarily offered again, and one should not procrastinate when they do show up. It was a big decision for the family. They were now responsible for three boys; Joseph was thirteen, Gabriel nine and Paul was eight years old. But the dice was thrown and they looked ahead with some fear and excitement to the unknown.

A week later, Csipogo and Carolyn were booked for a two-night stay at the Sheraton Hotel in downtown San Francisco and were scheduled the next day at Bechtel Headquarters to undergo medical examination and listen to presentations on the customs of Saudi Arabia together with a roomful of other employees on their way to the kingdom, where Bechtel employees already numbered close to two thousand.

They had the afternoon free to wonder the streets of San Francisco and taste the tidbits the many stalls had to offer at the Fisherman's Wharf. Walking the steep incline of the street back to the hotel, Csipogo suddenly felt a sharp pain in the right side of his abdomen and felt dizzy. Carolyn quickly called a taxi, and they were driven to the nearest emergency at Mount Zion Jewish hospital. The attending physician happened to be a Hungarian

FIND A PLACE TO CALL HOME

doctor and he was quickly attended to. He underwent physical examination, blood tests, and x-rays.

"I suspect appendicitis, but the blood tests are inconclusive. I recommend that you see your family doctor right away, when you return to Canada," the doctor told him, and he was released.

Csipogo was now concerned that he may not pass the Bechtel medical examination. He didn't mention the abdominal pain and passed the exams. Back in Canada, he was rushed to St. Joseph Hospital with a burst appendix. Fate was once again kind to him; his body formed a protective mass barrier that prevented an internal infection. The recovery delayed their departure for a month, but then they were on their way to London and Athens via British Airways and the Saudi Airline to Riyadh.

In Athens they had lined up at the Saudi Airline counter and experienced their first cultural shock. Saudi citizens would not line up; they pushed ahead of everyone else. When the family finally got to the counter, they were told the plane was full.

"We have reservations," Carolyn protested vehemently, but it was of no avail. They were a big family, and it freed up five seats for Saudi nationals. But they were assigned luxury hotel accommodation at the Athens Intercontinental with all expenses paid.

Carolyn was in a vindictive mood and ordered the most expensive items on the menu with a high-priced bottle of wine.

"Carolyn, I don't think the airline will pay for the wine."

"They better," and that is all she said.

After dinner, when they were returning to their room, four pilots in the uniform of Saudi Airline stepped inside the elevator.

"Are you with Saudia?" Carolyn asked.

"Yes, the plane did not take off. We experienced mechanical problems."

"What happened to all the passengers?" Carolyn inquired.

"They will have to spend the night at the airport. They couldn't find hotel accommodation for all the passengers."

"Now I feel good," Carolyn remarked as the pilots looked at her inquiringly.

Two Boeing 747 planes flown in the next day accommodated all the passengers. As they disembarked at the Riyadh airport, Joseph was leading the way down the stairs to the tarmac. He seemed perplexed, looking around as if disoriented, waving his hand in the air.

"I thought the heat came from the engines, but it is not, it is all around us," he said.

The temperature must have been close to fifty degrees Centigrade, and it was a great relief to enter the air-conditioned terminal building. There were live flower arrangements throughout the building, and it was beautiful. The children were stunned by the colorful display and quickly forgot the heat outside that they will have to cope with for the next four years.

"I have never seen so many flowers indoors," Paul remarked.

"They are flown in from Amsterdam weekly," a stewardess in KLM Royal Dutch Airline uniform walking by told him.

"Hurry up boys, we have to go through passport control, find our luggage, and catch the flight to Dhahran," Carolyn urged them on.

The sun was setting on the horizon when they disembarked at the Dhahran airport. Dave and his wife, Florence, were waiting for them in the terminal building and loaded their few belongings in the trunk of their car.

"Jubail is some one hundred miles north from here on a four-lane highway, so relax and enjoy the view. It is nighttime, but you will be surprised. It will be almost like driving in broad daylight as the road is lit and the power poles with fluorescent lights are placed half the distance apart to what we are used to in North America," Dave told them.

It was Joseph who noticed the numerous car wrecks on the side of the road in both directions.

"Why are these wrecks not cleared away?" Joseph asked.

"Well, the Saudis put their fate in the hands of Allah and drive their Mercedes cars at one hundred miles per hour. The wrecks are left on the road to remind Saudi drivers to slow down," Dave said.

"What are those bright lights on the right off in the distance?" Joseph asked.

"That is the Ras Tanura oil refinery and port facility. Most of the oil produced in the Eastern Province of Saudi Arabia is shipped to the world from this port," Dave explained.

Soon the bright lights of Jubail appeared on the horizon and large earth-moving vehicles could be seen parked everywhere.

"Before anything could be built, a smooth, stable surface had to be created. Vast amount of earth had to be moved: nearly four hundred million cubic meters or enough earth to make a band nine meters wide and one meter high around the equator. They also dredged the full length of the ocean floor around the planned city perimeter and ten kilometer into the sea for construction of a deep water port facility," Dave explained.

"We are now driving on the coastal boulevard of Jubail along the temporary camps that were erected to house the expatriate staff involved with the project; camps 7, 8, 9, 10 and camp 11 called HAII AL HUWAYLAT. Camps for single workers, mainly from third-world countries had been built on the north edge of the industrial development. They are more truly camp structures. What you see here are three-bedroom manufactured homes in all the camps, except camp 11 which consist of precast concrete structures. The manufactured houses are temporary homes and will eventually be dismantled, except camp 11. AL HUWAYLAT has a modern hospital, staffed with British, Scottish, and Indian doctors and nurses and is reputed to be a very safe hospital. Saudi nationals have free access to medical care and drugs, and Bechtel employees will have the same privileges. So your health insurance will be useful to you only when you are outside of the kingdom. Surprisingly, in many respects, the kingdom is more of a welfare state than the so-called socialist countries as money from the oil wealth is allowed to trickle down to the general population. The seven thousand members of the ruling royal family may have an extravagant lifestyle, but the government also imparts many benefits to the citizens unavailable in other countries. Jubail is also a good example of how money is invested by the government in the future of the country. You are lucky you have been assigned a house in camp 11, right across from the Bechtel project manager's house and on the street of the *Royal Commission Guest Houses*. It is a four-bedroom house with four bathrooms: two eastern bathrooms and two western bathrooms. Some British expatriates used their eastern bathrooms to ferment wine from grapes in huge glass bottles. You can buy grapes in the grocery store, but you can not buy alcohol anywhere in the country. They were expelled from the kingdom because their fermentation bottles blew up and were found out. So don't say, I didn't warn you!" Dave said and laughed.

"Something else I have to warn you about," Dave continued.

"Don't ever make your wife mad at you. Women are not allowed to drive in Saudi Arabia. If the wife is caught driving, it is the husband who goes to jail. You are responsible for the behavior of your household."

"What is that huge place along the seashore?" the children asked, looking at the brightly lit massive compound in amazement.

"That is the local palace for the king and his entourage when visiting the city. The king maintains several palaces all over the country," Dave informed them.

"How often does he come here?" Joseph asked.

"He may come once or twice a year for a couple of days. But it is fully staffed all year around," Dave told him smiling.

The boulevard was wide, lined with palm trees and an even wider pedestrian walkway on both sides of the road, planted with flowering oleanders and flame trees.

"The palm trees and flowering trees and bushes had all been imported. Some five hundred million dollars had been spent already on landscaping alone. A desalination plant provides drinking water to the houses, and the discharged gray water from the homes goes through a filtration process, and then it is reused for irrigation. Each of the trees and plants has three small underground plastic tubes brought to them, providing dripping water. A backup water truck is driven around daily, and the driver monitors the health of the plants as the plastic tubes occasionally get plugged by sand during sandstorms. All the plants are tracked by name and location in a data base. One of the ornamental trees, a beautiful yellow tree called the *Jew tree* caused a real stir with the Royal Commission and Bechtel was told to remove all the *Jew trees*. But as there were hundreds of them already planted and thriving, a compromise was agreed to: no more *Jew trees* will be planted, and the existing ones will be renamed in the data base to *Yellow Arbor*. Since plants have been introduced the bird population has increased noticeably, and they are just as colorful as the plants," Dave told the boys.

"Cooling water for the industrial plants is also obtained from the sea and is distributed in inflow and outflow channels, and it is cooled and filtered before it is returned to the sea. Great emphasis is placed here to protect the environment and have a sustainable process in place. Black water from the homes is held in sedimentation ponds and treated before it is returned to the sea," Dave continued.

The sign ALL HUWAILAT came into view, and they made a left hand turn onto a beautifully landscaped street with large impressive homes painted all white, like something out of Greece.

"Well, yours is not quite that luxurious, those are the Royal Commission Guest Houses, but yours is nice too. Here we are" as they turned into a carport.

The house had two entrances and Dave had to explain.

"Camp 11 is a permanent settlement, and the houses are built to Saudi lifestyle. They have separate entrances and separate living rooms for male and female guests, and the six-foot-high fence serves to shield the woman from prying eyes.

The separation of sexes is very strict in Saudi society. Men and women don't play sports together. Schools for boys and girls are being built at opposite ends of the city. There are separate hours for swimming at the pool for girls and boys. Your house is fully furnished with brand-new furniture from South Carolina. Welcome to Saudi Arabia."

"Thanks Dave for everything. This is more than any man could ask for," Csipogo said, overwhelmed.

"Well, I must say I had to fight hard for you. Mr. Mubarak the Saudi project manager wanted to get somebody else when you didn't show up on time. He didn't think appendectomy is a good enough reason to be a month late."

"Have a good night's rest and see you in the office at the Royal Commission Administration building, which is just a short walking distance to the north from here. You can't miss it when you see it. It is still under construction, but we moved in anyway," Dave said.

The administration building had not yet been painted on the outside and it had the grayish color of concrete. It had the appearance of a castle in need of repair. But on the inside it was luxurious. Csipogo felt he had just entered an open-concept resort hotel in Hawaii. The reception lobby was all shining marble and was decorated with tropical plants. It had open space to the roof, and the balconies lead to open-concept offices on the upper floors.

Dave introduced him to the other members of the department.

"Robert Kelly and Larry Hollis look after outside plant and central office switching respectively, and you will be responsible for everything else, which includes interoffice trunks, microwave radio connection to Saudi Telephone, television distribution to homes on coaxial cable, emergency communication for police, fire, and ambulance services, and the paging system. Continental Telephones of USA is our consultant on the project, and they are represented on site by Mr. Gault and Mr. Savage. We also have two Saudi engineers in training: Abdullah Bukhari and Fouad Al Zayer. Fouad just returned from his studies in the United States, and he will be your counterpart for the duration of the project. Transfer of knowledge is part of our responsibilities. Bechtel is basically charged with project management responsibility on behalf of the Saudi Royal Commission."

Csipogo and Fouad became close friends over the four years, and for Csipogo, it was an interesting experience to watch the transformation of a young Saudi returning from the United States and reintegrating into Saudi society.

In the beginning Fouad was like any American teenager. He came to work in shirt and jeans he had got used to wearing in college in the United States. After about six months, the peer pressure had got to him, and he changed to traditional Saudi clothing when attending meetings with other Saudis. He had a girlfriend in the United States and left his Mercedes car with her as he intended to return to America. After about two years, he wore the Saudi *thawb* and *gutra* all the time and his family introduced him to a local girl from his birthplace of Qatif. And in the third year, he was getting married, and Csipogo and Carolyn were invited to his wedding.

Csipogo teased him about that.

"Fouad, did you just lose a Mercedes?"

"Yes, I did," and he laughed.

But Csipogo never saw the bride during the wedding ceremony. The men held the celebration in Qatif and the women in Al Khobar some twenty miles apart.

He did see her after their honeymoon when they visited him in his home. She had entered covered in black *abaya*, threw the garment with some disdain in the corner on the floor and a gorgeous young girl emerged dressed in the latest Parisian fashion in high-heeled shoes.

Since women were not allowed to drive, Bechtel put several mini-buses at the disposal of the Bechtel wives with full-time Saudi drivers on standby. One such driver was Abdullah, who was known for having two wives. The favorite hangout for the Bechtel wives were the *gold suqs of Al Khobar*. Abdullah, on these trips was busy too, loading not gold but large sacks of rice for the family. Two families to look after was not really a voluntary choice made by him; he inherited the second family. His older brother died, and by tradition it became his responsibility to care for his brother's family.

Bechtel also built a golf course for the women in the desert. It had no grass, so the players had to carry an artificial green mat to place the ball on for each strike. And the greens were carefully pressed down sand circles. Occasionally players forgot to pick up their green mats, and running back, questioned the group behind them, "Have you seen my grass?"

The obstacles on the golf course were palm trees, often with snakes curled up in the shade of the undergrowth. So it could become a hazardous exercise to retrieve balls. And free roaming camels had the habit of taking a sand bath on the greens, making putting challenging.

Fouad during one of his visits, promised Csipogo to take him and the family to the famous camel market in Hofuf. Until 1953 Hofuf had been the administrative capital of the Al-Hasa Province, but in that year it was moved to Dammam on the Arabian Gulf, and the official name of the area was changed to Eastern Province. Hofuf is still the administrative center of the Oasis. It has a huge open-market, and camels are brought there hobbled in the back of huge trucks equipped with forklifts, and the unloading of screaming camels is quite a site to see. They are all legs, head, and enormous eyes. Csipogo walked up to a baby camel, still hobbled on the ground, and patted him on the forehead, quite unaware that camels have the habit of biting strangers. A young Saudi came rushing at him with a big smile on his face, shook Csipogo's hands, talking excitedly in Arabic.

Csipogo looked helplessly at Fouad.

"What is he saying, Fouad?"

"He is congratulating you. He thinks it is a sign from Allah that you should become the owner of that camel because it didn't bite you."

"And just what am I going to do with a camel?" Csipogo asked.

"You should buy it and let it loose on the Bechtel golf course," Fouad teased him.

"That is just what I am going to do, you smart-ass American teenager," Csipogo retorted.

Fouad and Csipogo both liked swimming laps in the Al Huwailat pool for exercise and did it twice a week during their lunch breaks. After swimming laps, they spread themselves to the hot noontime sun-rays, quite unaware of the dangers of skin cancer. On one occasion, they witnessed a touching scene, where two young Saudi boys led a very old toothless and blind man, probably their grandfather, to the edge of the pool and made him touch the water, explaining to him what it was. He had probably never seen a swimming pool in his life-time.

"Our grandparents lived a hardy life. They didn't have air-conditioned homes, walked or rode on camel back long distances in the hot sun and sandstorms and probably never saw a doctor or dentist in their life time. That is why you see in Saudi Arabia a lot of old men blind and toothless. Our generation lives in air-conditioned homes, sits around watching TV and lost the Bedouin toughness. We would not survive in the fifty degrees Celsius heat in the desert. That old man, blind and toothless, could probably still walk from Jubail to Ras Tanura in the noon heat if you held his hands," Fouad said.

Csipogo was an experienced sailor, and Fouad wanted to learn sailing and he bought a catamaran. The two of them took the boat out for a trial run along the dredged channel. Sailing a catamaran in strong wind is exciting, gliding on one pontoon and the other out of the water. It took them only an hour to get far away from the shore and when the wind died; it took them eight hours to get back. With dwindling water supply in the burning sun, it became a dreaded trek back. They were close to shore when a hammerhead shark suddenly surfaced near the boat. After reporting this shark sighting, it became a Royal Commission-approved policy to install protective nets around areas designated for public swimming.

In Jubail nothing was built unless it was part of the *Master Plan*. Open channel storm sewers, like those in Phoenix Arizona, were in the master plan. But the Royal Commission objected to these being in the plan and ordered them removed, arguing that it had not rained in Jubail in one hundred years. That year unusual monsoon rains hit the area, and large lakes formed in the desert that didn't dry up for months. Power manholes and communication manholes filled up with water. Some streets became impassable. There were power outages, and one after the other, the cable television amplifiers under the salty water in the manholes failed, interrupting television service to the homes. This proved to be the last straw, as the Saudi wives started phoning their husbands at work about loosing the TV signal.

The Deputy Director General for Jubail Mr. Ibrahim Al-Mubarek phoned the Bechtel project manager Jim Moe, "We give up. Tell your God to stop the deluge, and we will reinstate the storm sewers in the *Mastor Plan.*"

The *International School* the children attended was an all-American curriculum school with all-American teachers and nearly all of the students were the children of Bechtel employees. It was an unusual school, where no one had failing marks; they were exceptionally smart students. The school had an excellent library with a full-time librarian. The music class provided the students with whatever instrument they wanted to play and allowed them to take it home. It catered to students up to grade 8, after which they had to leave Saudi Arabia and attend *International School* elsewhere of their choice, with all expenses covered by the Saudi government. Soccer and baseball was the main after school sport activity and Bechtel fathers volunteered as coaches. The teams had girls as well as boys until large number of Saudi men started to show up to watch the girls swing the bat. The Saudi religious police soon showed up to end this digression and prohibited the girls playing with the boys. Csipogo was coaching soccer, and he had two girls on his team, and it was heartbreaking to tell the tearful girls that they can't continue playing on the team. It was this select Jubail team that beat, that year, the eleven to twelve year old boy's team of Aramco from Dahran to a score of 2:1.

In 1984 the Iran-Iraq war was already in its fourth year, and it became a vicious war of attrition, which threatened the entire gulf area. The Saudi air force was on constant alert, and F-15

FIND A PLACE TO CALL HOME

jets regularly patrolled the sky over Jubail. Being on the Police, Fire, and Ambulance Committee, Csipogo was well aware of the dangers Jubail faced. The massive tank farm holding both gas and oil feedstock, if attacked by aircraft, could have resulted in an explosion of several atomic bombs in magnitude, and evacuation plans were in-place that were subject to the direction of the wind. On one lunch-break, Carolyn complained that the TV screen is *snowy*. Csipogo dutifully climbed the ladder to the roof to readjust the VHF TV antenna. The pilot of an F-15 jet decided to investigate what this foreigner was doing on the roof, and the roar from the engine, as the plane pulled up again to join three others in the sky, nearly deafened our master TV repairman. The planes then headed off in the direction of the sea. In less than five minutes, Csipogo heard a massive explosion and could see an aircraft engulfed in flames falling into the sea. He learned later that an Iranian phantom jet invaded the Saudi air-space and was shot down. And there were no further attempts by Iran to invade Saudi air-space and possibly trigger the entry of Saudi Arabia and other gulf states into the war.

The Bechtel ladies of the Whispering Sands Golf Club were a hardy bunch. After having been toughened by the conditions in the Saudi desert, they now lifted their eyes to adventures farther afield, and in February of 1986 they signed up for a nine-day tour of Egypt: twenty women and one man, and his name was Moses. They flew to Cairo and spent their first night at the luxurious Cairo Sheraton Heliopolis. Here a tour guide joined them the next day, and they flew on to Luxor. In Luxor they boarded a floating luxury hotel the *MS Aton* and cruised upstream on the Nile River. They visited all the world famous sites of antiquities without fatalities: the Karnak and Luxor Temples, the Necropolis of Thebes, the Valley of the Kings, Queens and Nobles, Esna Temple of Khnum, Edfu Temple of Horus, Kom Ombo Temple of Sobek, the Temple of Ramses II and the Temple of his chief wife Queen Nefertiti. Their problems started when they returned to Cairo on the seventh day. Their travel itinerary included a visit to the Cairo Museum of Antiquities and a tour of the famous

Pyramids of Giza, the Sphinx, and its Valley Temple. But two days earlier, a serious riot broke out in Cairo. The entire police force went on strike for higher wages. The army was called out and there were armed clashes, and many buildings in the city were on fire. The museum was closed, and touring the Pyramids was out of the question. Not according the Bechtel ladies. They pointed to their written contract. And never underestimate the power of twenty women. The Travel Agency hired an army tank to escort their tour bus to the Pyramids of Giza. Moses led the twenty women to Egypt, and after nine days, successfully led them out of Egypt, and the Travel Agency was relieved to see them gone.

By the fall of 1986, at the end of Csipogo's contract for the project, all communication facilities were in place in the Industrial area, the Camps and Al-Huwaylat, and construction of the first phase of the permanent residential area (Al-Fanateer) had been completed.

Csipogo, over the four years, witnessed the transformation of Saudis coming from traditional somewhat haphazard Saudi villages and adjusting to life in a planned city where they were not allowed the killing and bleeding of a goat in the sand and did it in the bathtub instead. But he also witnessed Saudis starting to take pride in the orderliness of Jubail. On one occasion, when the driver of an earth-moving truck threw an empty coke bottle out the window, the man in the white *thawb* revved his Mercedes after him and ordered him to go back and pick up the offending can. He learned the power of the *shamal* that can remove the paint from a Chevrolet in two years. He learned to appreciate shade, watching baseball sitting in the narrow projection of a palm tree and appreciate the role plants can play in changing the desert into a blooming oasis teaming with birds. He learned that you can spend billions on sending two men on a useless trip to the moon or build a flowering oasis in the desert here on earth. He was greatly impressed by the efforts the Saudi Government demonstrated on the Jubail project to protect and improve the environment and spare no money to

FIND A PLACE TO CALL HOME

do so. He learned to play golf on a golf course that has not a square inch of grass on it and about the extremes people would go to get alcohol if you prohibit it. Most of all, he learned that friendship conquers all differences.

On his return to Canada, Csipogo brought with him two traditional Saudi headgears: the red and white checkered *ghutra* and gave one to Victor, his Italian friend and skiing partner. Victor's fertile brain went to work right away, and he suggested that they wear it during their spring skiing at Mt. Baker in Washington State, just to see what the reaction to it will be. To their surprise, people were very polite and ushered them ahead at the lineup to the lift, and they overheard people whispering behind them: "They must be members of the Saudi Royal family."

Unfortunately, on the slope, Victor ran into his Jewish dentist, and Victor greeted him enthusiastically, "Salam Alaikum." His Jewish dentist became very agitated and simply turned away from him.

His Majesty King Fahd Ibn Abdul Aziz

Earth Moving Equipment

The Tank Farm

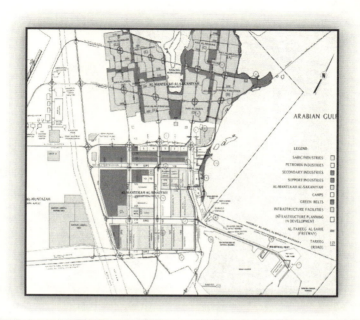

The input/output cooling saltwater channels in the industrial area in Jubail.

The Royal Commission Administration Building under construction in Jubail.

The palm trees in Al-Huwaylat.

Even the street signs had to be cleaned.

The offending Jew Tree

The bedouin.

Inside the Administration Building

Appreciating shade

Hall-Al Lulu Ballfield Spring 1983

The Flame Trees

The power of *shamal*.

AT THE CAMEL MARKET   HOFUF SAUDI ARABIA 1983

The champions of Jubail

Traditional Saudi feast...on the floor

The home in Al-Huwaylat, Jubail

Fouad's ceremonial wedding march through the city of Quatif

Two Saudi Princes

CHAPTER 8

Indonesia

It was a warm and sunny summer day in Vancouver in 1991 when Carolyn unexpectedly uttered something that surprised her husband.

"Aren't we going somewhere soon?"

"What do you mean? Are you anxious to pack again?" Csipogo asked.

"No, I am only amazed that the gypsy in you was able to stay in one place for more than five years."

The next day, something totally unexpected happened. Csipogo was called to the office of the manager of B.C. Telephones human resources.

"You have more international experience than anyone I know in this company. Would you like to go to Indonesia? Our subsidiary Canac Microtel got a contract to design and manage the construction of a digital microwave radio route across the Island of Sumatra, and they are looking for a radio engineer. You would be on loan to them from us. The Asian Development Bank is funding the project."

"Let me ask my wife. Can I use your phone?"

"Carolyn, would you like to go to Indonesia?"

"Are you nuts?"

FIND A PLACE TO CALL HOME

"Just as I suspected, she agreed."

"When do I start?"

"Well it is kind of urgent. The rest of the team is already there. Can you leave next week?"

"Well, my children are old enough to stay in the house on their own and my wife and I, we can be ready."

When he arrived home, Carolyn received him in a very agitated mood.

"You are truly out of your mind this time. We can't leave our sons alone in the house. They will burn the place down."

"Joseph is twenty-two, Gabriel is eighteen, and Paul is seventeen. It is a great time for them to be on their own. Imagine, they will have to learn to cook and get along with each-other," Csipogo countered.

"That is true. But I think it will come as a big shock to them."

When they told the boys later that day what is awaiting them, they danced across the room in a gay outburst.

"Well, this is not what your mother expected, you rascals. She thought you would cry and protest."

"No, we are happy for you. You will love Indonesia. And it is time for the two of you to be on your own."

Well, if that wasn't a turn of the tables, Csipogo thought.

Only a week later, Csipogo and Carolyn were in possession of airline tickets with Singapore Airlines to fly from Vancouver to Singapore and onto Medan on the Island of Sumatra, Indonesia.

They had been to Singapore before on one of their holiday excursions from Saudi Arabia. It was a much greater contrast then, coming from the desert and landing in what from the air looked like a tropical paradise. They stayed overnight at the Four Seasons hotel, which was an overnight experience of ultimate luxury and caught their connecting flight to Medan the next day.

Indonesia is an archipelago of some 17,500 islands. It lies alongside the equator and has a tropical climate with two distinct wet and dry seasons. The average daily temperatures vary between twenty-six and thirty degrees Centigrade. With 238 million people it is the world's fourth most populous country, and has the world's largest population of Muslims. Approximately 85 percent of Indonesians are Muslims, 9 percent of the population is Christian, 3 percent Hindu and 2 percent Buddhist and other. Approximately 58 percent of the population lives on the Island of Java, the world's most populous island. The country has extensive natural resources that include oil, gas, tin, copper, gold and lumber and tourism of course. Bali is a natural paradise and attracts a large number of tourists each year. Despite its large population and densely populated regions, Indonesia has vast areas of wilderness that supports the world's second highest biodiversity after Brazil. Forests cover approximately 60 percent of the country. It is situated on the edges of the Pacific, Eurasian, and Australian tectonic plates, which makes it a site of high seismic and volcanic activity. Indonesia has at least 150 active volcanoes that include Krakatoa and Tambora, both famous for their devastating eruptions. Across its many islands, Indonesia consists of distinct ethnic, linguistic, and religious groups. The Javanese are the largest and politically dominant ethnic group. Following three and a half centuries of Dutch colonialism, Indonesia secured its independence after World War II with Sukarno as its first President.

Sumatra is the world's fifth largest island and the third largest in Indonesia. The island runs approximately 1790 kilometers northwest to southeast, crossing the equator near the center. At its widest point, the island spans 435 kilometers. The island is dominated by two geographical regions, the Barisan Mountains in the west and swampy plains in the east.

The largest city is Medan with a population of approximately 1,770,000.

The Canac/Microtel team was temporarily housed at the Danau Toba Hotel in the center of the city. The taxi had brought Csipogo and Carolyn from the airport to the front of the hotel. Csipogo was the first to get out of the vehicle and instantly two young Indonesian women in long flowing dress surrounded him and led him away.

"Sorry ladies, but there is a small problem . . . my wife," Csipogo protested.

"It is OK. we don't mind," the ladies chimed.

Carolyn used more convincing language.

"He is mine, scatter!"

Csipogo learned later that he was not the only one awarded this friendly reception on arrival.

The hotel was a lively place with a Batak group playing dance music every night. They regularly invited requests from the audience and encouraged the patrons to sing along with them, which created an enjoyable atmosphere. One of the favorites was a drinking song that was the group's theme song, '*Le Soi, Le Soi . . .*'

Batak is a collective term used to identify a number of ethnic groups predominantly found in North Sumatra. The term includes Toba, Karo, Pakpuk, Simalungun, Angkola, and Mandailing, each of which is distinct but related group with distinct, albeit related, languages and customs. The Batak are mostly Christian with a Muslim minority and are most prominent in the north highlands around Lake Toba. Their homes are wood structures with elaborate artistic carvings, very distinctly Batak. Some communities, even today, practice matriarchal rule, where the female is in charge, and when the man finds his suitcase on the doorsteps, it means he is done, no longer wanted.

Lake Toba in North Sumatra is easily the largest lake in Southeast Asia (30 by 100 kilometers) and one of the deepest in the world at 450 meters. Lake Toba was formed as a result of a gigantic volcanic explosion. In the middle of the lake lies Samosir Island that is basically a resurgent dome. Today it is a very popular tourist destination, with pine trees and clean beaches, with balmy, cooler tropical temperatures, that comes with the higher elevation.

The Toba eruption was a supervolcanic eruption that had occurred around seventy thousand years ago. It is recognized as one of the Earth's largest known eruptions. This event plunged the planet into a six-to-ten-year volcanic winter and possibly an additional one-thousand-year cooling episode. This change in temperature resulted in the world's human population being reduced to to ten thousand or possibly a mere one thousand breeding pairs, creating a bottleneck in human evolution. Estimates of the eruptive volume vary between two thousand and three thousand cubic kilometers, of which approximately eight hundred cubic kilometers was deposited as ash fall. It deposited an ash layer fifteen centimeters thick over the entirety of South Asia. Volcanic deposit around Lake Toba itself is some four hundred meters deep, making it very fertile land. In comparison to the Toba eruption, Krakatoa, with its tens of thousands of deaths in 1883, was just a tiny belch. The May 1980 eruption of Mount St. Helens produced a mere 1 cubic kilometer of ash. Ice-core records from Greenland confirm that the one-thousand-year cold period was directly generated by the Toba eruption and may have triggered the last glaciations. The suns rays only weakly reached the ground all around the globe; plants received too little light. The average temperature dropped to five degrees Celsius, so that summers turned to winter and winters became deadly.

Today we know that humans and their near relatives survived this global Armageddon by nature in small groups, mainly in Africa. Genetic evidence suggests that all humans alive today, despite their apparent variety, are descended from a very small population, around seventy thousand years ago. It has been suggested that hominid populations, such as Homo erectus and Homo florescence on Flores, survived because they were upwind from the Toba eruption.

The first burst of business activity for the Canadian group was to find housing accommodations and office space. There were plenty of vocal locals offering to help and find houses. But they soon learned to avoid them. Their helpful assistance only increased the price. These helpers were known as the street hawkers '*looking for money.*' It is a well known phrase in Indonesia; men go out to look for money . . . not for a job. The Canadians quickly learned to do things without help.

The team that was charged with finding housing accommodation stumbled upon a walled-off compound on the edge of the city called Taman Setia Budi Indah, where the entire group was able to find housing accommodation at reasonable prices.

Csipogo, with another engineer, were charged with finding office space. First they went on a fishing trip, cautiously assessing what the prices were. They established that the going price in general was around $11 per square meter of floor space or higher. Then they approached the Chinese manager of a bank building they considered the best choice for their needs and offered him $10 per square meter. He reluctantly agreed. Csipogo and Dr. Adrian, the building manager became close friends over the next three years and spent many joyful days on the golf courses and Chinese restaurants of Medan. He managed the building for his Chinese friend, who owned the bank, the building, and palm oil and rubber plantations. But by training, he was really a medical doctor and practiced his trade in the evening hours between 5:00 PM and 7:00 PM. After a golf game and over a glass of beer, Dr. Adrian confessed to Csipogo that the price they had in mind was $13 per square meter, but starting with a low offer upfront was a clever maneuver by the two men negotiating team as this made him believe that someone had offered them office space for that price. Csipogo just smiled.

Once they had settled in the office, the real work began. The first step was to determine what frequency plan the radio system should operate on without interfering with existing systems. It soon became obvious that a new band will have to be used to avoid clashes with existing sites. Approval was obtained from ITU to use the newly released 5 gigahertz band with forty megahertz separation between channels to carry seven synchronous STM-1 channels that will be the ultimate capacity of the system. A tender document was prepared in cooperation with the Indonesian Post and Telecom central planners in Bandung that specified all the requirements in detail: existing towers, new towers required, tower heights, required antenna heights, sites with space diversity, sites without space diversity, site layouts, equipment room layouts, multiplexing plan, performance requirements, network management requirements. The tender document was highly praised by all the bidding companies (Alcatel, NEC, Fujitsu, Siemens, Nortel . . .) that it was clear and precise and it made their job of bidding easy.

The early survey works involved a lot of traveling from Banda Aceh in the north to Palembang in the south, to survey the new sites and familiarize with existing sites, crossing rivers on small ferries pulled by ropes across the river, driving on muddy forestry roads in the jungle and in the mountains. On one such jungle road the vehicle on which Csipogo and his Indonesian counter part engineers from Bandung were traveling got stuck in the mud, and they decided to walk the rest of the way to locate the selected new site. Soon they ran into a herd of elephants that marched across the road, and further down tiger excrement's were spotted in the middle of the road. Csipogo never experienced such nervousness. They had no guns, only maps and a GPS. His Indonesian companions thought nothing of it; they chatted and laughed all the way but formed a tight protective circle around Csipogo.

Fate is nearly always unpredictable. Csipogo's favorite city was Banda Aceh, with its impressive Grand Mosque, beautiful Lok Nga Beach, Weh Island across the water in the Andaman Sea and year around nearly constant temperature around twenty-seven degrees Celsius. And just ten years later on the twenty-sixth of December 2004, a massive underwater 9.3 earthquake struck only 155 miles off the coast of Banda Aceh in the Andaman Sea, and it killed some 170,000 people and left nearly 500,000 homeless in Banda Aceh and its surrounding.

On the Medan Golf and Country Club, free-roaming chickens were in abundance. Fried chicken was also the tastiest meal served in the restaurant. Csipogo was curious and asked the girl serving them, just who those chickens on the golf course belong to.

"Anyone who can catch them," was her answer.

Beside each tee-off mound entrepreneurial vendors set up small boutiques that offered drinks and fresh fruits. During one of their outings on the weekend, walking up to the tenth tee, Csipogo felt dizzy and saw two balls simmering at his foot on the tee. Dr Adrian recognized the problem right away.

"You are dehydrated. You need a drink and a banana."

The vendors were two young girls, may be seventeen years old. They made him sit in the shade and surrounded him on two sides.

"You look nice. I love your lips, they are thin, not wide like on our native men," one on the right commented.

"I want your baby," the other on the left announced and put her arms around him.

Csipogo swallowed the banana and nearly choked on it. He quickly returned to the tee box and hit the ball with a revitalized vision.

Around water hazards, young boys maybe ten years old loiter, and on the splash of the golf ball five boys dive looking for it. The asking price is fifty cents for a retrieved ball. The water is black and murky; it is a major miracle how these boys remain healthy.

The fairways also harbored small blood suckers in considerable numbers. One inexperienced blood sucker attached itself to the top of Dr. Adrian's golf ball, and he sent the poor thing soaring with a number 3 iron.

Csipogo's friendship with Dr. Adrian introduced him to the Chinese-Indonesian conflict. The Chinese were basically the wealthy class. They worked harder and were willing to put in long working hours. Indonesians were more laid back, less industrious, and they resented the Chinese domination of the economy. Chinese were not allowed into government jobs or enter university, these institutions were reserved for the military, so the Chinese gravitated to business and used and some misused the cheap Indonesian labor. When labor disputes broke out, it often turned into a massacre of Chinese, and the army had to step in to reestablish order. Chinese-language papers were closed by government proclamation and all Chinese religious expressions had to be confined to their homes. Chinese-language schools were phased out. Chinese script in public places was banned. Dr.

Adrian was mortally afraid of the army, and when the military had tournaments on the golf course, he refused to play.

"I was accepted to university only because I had an Indonesian sounding name," he told Csipogo.

Corruption was an institutionalized process in Indonesia. The end result was always poor workmanship. The country never got the best telephone, power, irrigation, or road systems. It nearly always got the worst because the Corporation offering the worst usually offered the highest bribes. The countries infrastructure was built on a system where ten percent of the money was siphoned off on every project at the very top and all the way down to the pauper ditch diggers. Even these poor laborers paid a percentage of their salary to some agent or territorial controller, who supposedly got them the job. It was an oppressive military dictatorship, where the government, the military, the police, and a small minority of superrich held all the power and comforts of life, and sixty percent of the population worked for less than four thousand rupiah a day (US$2 per day). They even defended the practice of low minimum wages in leading Indonesian newspapers as necessary to enable Indonesia to compete in the world markets. Europe too, they said, had to go through the industrial revolution sweatshops to advance to greatness. And the problem wormed its way into the world's leading lending institutions, like the World Bank and the Asian Development Bank. They abandoned their strict principles for zero tolerance for corruption and bribery on projects funded by them. They replaced it with a pragmatic approach of closing their eyes to it in the interest of keeping the flow of loans to countries with well-known corrupt practices as long as they were good customers and repaid their loans. Leading political figures of western nations also chose to ignore corruption in the interest of trade promotion. The Canadian consulting group paid highly for their mistake of not recognizing these facts of life as the project progressed.

Csipogo had a German engineer friend Bernd who managed a boiler factory, building large industrial boilers for palm oil and rubber factories. One day, he discovered that some of his workers were steeling steel plates used in the manufacturing of boilers and reported it to the local police chief. The police chief arrived at the factory in his Volvo wagon and asked who the thieves were. He pointed them out.

"One thousand US dollars," the police chief announced and held his hand out.

After being paid he hauled the workers off to the local jail. Within a week the family of the prisoners returned the stolen plates. The factory manager was satisfied; he fired the workers but didn't press charges. The next day, the family returned crying in his office. They told him the police chief wants one thousand US dollars to release the prisoners.

And he paid one thousand dollars the second time.

Csipogo and Carolyn experienced the corruption in Indonesia at the Medan airport. Indonesia had an exit tax when exiting the country of 250,000 rupiah per person (US$125). Csipogo handed the man behind the counter ten crisp 50,000 rupiah notes, carefully bundled together. The bundle of notes was lowered and then it came up again.

"It is 50,000 rupiah short," floated the voice across the small window.

Csipogo had no recourse; he had to come up with the missing 50,000 rupiah note, or ten percent bribe. Csipogo on subsequent trips, meticulously counted out the 50,000 rupiah notes one by one onto the clerk's desk, while looking the clerk straight in the eye.

Suharto ruled this country with an iron fist for thirty years and during his presidency, three out of five Indonesians earned less than US$2 per day. The Suharto family had an annual income that was estimated in the billions of US dollars.

In Indonesia they drive on the left side of the road, and there are no rules. Whoever gets there first owns the spot. It requires constant alertness to drive in rush hour traffic here. The Canadian team members were not allowed to drive during week days; the company hired local drivers to lessen the insurance costs. They did drive on weekends, on excursions to Berestagi to purchase fresh fruits and vegetables, to Lake Toba, to relax in the cooler highland temperatures and swim in the lake, and to the Bukit Lawang orangutan rehabilitation center to watch the feeding of the orangutans which were being reintroduced to the wild. On their visit to Bukit Lawang a large male orangutan suddenly climbed down from the feeding platform and embraced one of the wives. She didn't panic, but she was stunned.

"I guess I am beautiful," she announced bravely.

On his first year leave back to Vancouver, the very first morning, Csipogo woke early and decided to drive to the bank. He drove on the left side of the road until he came to a four-way intersection, and there he wondered why the car facing him was driving on the wrong side of the road. Only the menacing horn blown by the opposing car made him realize that it was him on the wrong side of the road.

On their return to Medan, they found that some uninvited guests had moved in to the attic. In Indonesia cats are free-roaming animals, and when they expect kittens, they seek a safe shelter. And they make an awful racket and usually at night.

"We have to round up those cats," Carolyn said after a sleepless night.

The next morning, when Carolyn went shopping, Csipogo thought he had a bright idea. He rounded up a ladder and put out food in a dish on the roof of the carport. As the mother cat approached the dish, Csipogo quickly grabbed her. But this was no ordinary house cat; she fought and scratched. Csipogo lost all reasoning and jumped on the roof to chase her. The roof was corrugated vinyl roof that collapsed under his weight, and he fell through the rafters, scratching his arms and breaking his collar bone in the process. Luckily he landed feet first on the concrete floor below. Cats are not his favorite animals ever since.

The office secretary for the Canadian group was a local hire, a very attractive Batak woman in her thirties, and she was getting married to her longtime boyfriend that year. The entire Canadian team was invited to the wedding as guests of honor. An Indonesian wedding is no ordinary event. Bataks are Christian, and the church ceremony was much like any Christian wedding, but what followed was quite something else. In Indonesia for the wedding reception, the entire street is blocked off to traffic. Several huge tents are put up on the street, and anyone walking by is welcome to drop in for a meal. They usually slaughter a whole cow. And there is lots of rice to go with it. And the rice just keeps coming. Invited women guests line up to the very corner of the street, and they all carry huge bags of rice on their head; it is a present to the bride. She must not go hungry in the first year of her marriage.

In Indonesia Csipogo learned to have a much greater appreciation and respect for this miracle grain of Southeast Asia. Ninety-two percent of the rice produced in the world comes from China, India, Indonesia, Pakistan, Bagladesh, Vietnam, Thailand, Myamar, Philippines and Japan. China, India, and Indonesia alone are responsible for more than half of the world output. Rice is vital for the nutrition of much of the population of Asia. The commonly accepted view is that rice was first domesticated from wild rice in the region of the Yangtze River in China. The earliest widely accepted date for cultivated rice is placed at around 2,500 to 3,000 BC. Rice production is well suited to tropical regions with low labor costs and high rainfall as it is very labor intensive to cultivate and requires ample water. It can be grown practically anywhere even on steep hills or mountains. Many countries consider rice as a strategic food staple, and various governments subject its trade to a wide range of controls and interventions. Only about five to six percent of the rice produced is traded internationally.

The fertile volcanic soil of the Indonesian archipelago and particularly Java and Bali made rice a central dietary staple for the country. Since fertilizers and pesticides are relatively expensive inputs, farmers typically plant seeds in a very small germinating plot first. Three weeks after germination the six to eight inch stalks are picked and replanted at greater separation in a larger plot in a backbreaking manual procedure, while standing in water. It is mainly cultivated by small farmers on holdings of less than one hectare. Rice farmers during the growing season are in constant battle with pests of all kinds; weeds, pathogens, insects and birds. Near harvesting time, farmers install all kinds of strings, scarecrows, whistles, and bells and sleep in the fields to discourage birds devastating their crops. Unmilled rice, known as paddy, is usually harvested when the grains have a moisture content of around 25 percent. Harvesting is usually carried out manually. Harvesting is followed by thrashing, either immediately or within a day or two. Again much of the thrashing is carried out by hand. Subsequently paddy needs to be dried to bring down the moisture content to no more than 20 percent for milling. Drying has to be carried out quickly to avoid formation of moulds. A familiar site in the country is paddy laid out to dry along the roads and post harvest losses can be quite high; some estimates put it as high as 40 percent.

Csipogo encouraged his children never to leave food on the plate to throw out. It was in Manila in the Philippines at a restaurant serving smorgasbord that Csipogo encountered an interesting experiment to discourage waste. The price of the smorgasbord was set at half price, but if the waiter noticed leftover on the plate the full price was charged.

In Indonesia the most common family transport is the motorcycle. It is not uncommon to see two adults and three children on a vehicle. One child would be sitting on the fuel tank in front of the driver and the wife on the back seat would be holding onto two children, one on her lap and the smallest on her back.

The most disturbing site on the road is to see the beggars at busy intersections. Usually they are lepers. They sit on the curb in the middle of the road and they are exposed to the fumes all day long. And in Indonesia, they still sell leaded gasoline.

During one of his field trips Csipogo got the shock of his life in a roadside restaurant just outside Palembang. He asked for the menu. And they brought out twenty-five dishes and placed them on the table in front of him.

"What are they trying to do to me?" Csipogo asked his Indonesian coworkers at the table.

"That is the menu. We will have to pay only for what we eat."

In their second year, Csipogo and Carolyn decided to spend their vacation locally and play golf in Thailand on the island of Phuket and the Genting Highlands of Malaysia, an hours drive from Kuala Lumpur.

They flew to Singapore and checked in at the Raffles Hotel. It is the most expensive hotel in Singapore, but they thought they can afford one night in the lap of luxury, and the Mariachis were performing nightly. But they didn't count on Michael Jackson being one of the guests, and it turned their stay there to an absolute mayhem with thousands of screaming fans outside the hotel.

Phuket is approximately the size of Singapore (540 square km), and it is Thailand's largest island. It is situated off the west coast of Thailand in the Andaman Sea. The island is connected to the mainland by two bridges at the north end. The island is mostly mountainous, but the western coast of the island has several of the most beautiful sandy beaches in the world. It is here that Csipogo and Carolyn checked in at the Kata Beach Resort Hotel.

Phuket has four 18 holes golf courses; the Phuket Golf and Country Club and the Blue Canyon Country Club are the best in Asia. Phuket attracts many foreigners and some 20 percent of the permanent residents on the island are foreigners. Csipogo and Carolyn teamed up with one such person during a game. He was a fisherman from Alaska. He worked six months in Alaska and lived six months in Phuket.

"What attract me here is the climate, the beautiful beaches, golf and the smiling faces of the people here. It is not without reason Thailand is called *The Land of Smiles*. And the cadies on the golf course are girls and you can ask for one or two."

The west coast beaches of Phuket were also heavily damaged by the same 2004 tsunami that destroyed Banda Aceh. As many as 250 people were reported dead, including many foreign tourists.

From Phuket, Csipogo and Carolyn flew to Kuala Lumpur, Malaysia and took a taxi to *Genting Highlands Resort*, which is approximately an hour's drive from the city. It is high up in the mountains and the climate here is pleasantly cool. The *Awana* golf course located here is another Asian jewel. The cadies are also girls here, but you can only have one. The hotel has a casino attached to it. So, after checking in, Csipogo headed for the golf course, and Carolyn headed for the casino.

Carolyn didn't show up till late the next morning.

"You mean you gambled all through the night?" Csipogo asked.

"Yes, and I lost all my money."

"You lost two thousand dollars?"

"I had a bad night."

"You have managed to ruin our vacation with this. Now we have to leave earlier."

When they returned to Medan, the bid documents were all in, and the critical work of evaluation began. Two of the bids were close in price, and after careful evaluation the Canac Microtel team unanimously recommended the higher bid. Their equipment was considered higher quality than that submitted by the lowest bid. Then the pressure tactics began. The Canac Microtel team was called to appear in Bandung at the Indonesian Post and Telecom Headquarters. First they were politely asked to change the recommendation. The Canadians tried to convince them that they are acting in the best interest of Indonesian Post and Telecom. The Indonesian engineering staff members, in private, admitted that they agreed with the recommendation, but they have orders from higher up to change it. The Canac Microtel team refused to change it, citing professional ethics. The Canadian team paid heavily for their stubbornness. Their contract was cancelled, and they were ordered out of the country. The Indonesian Post and Telecom invalidated the bidding process and invited a second round of Bids. Only the Bidder favored by the Indonesian Post and Telecom submitted a bid the second time, the other companies refused to do so. The Asian Development Bank remained silent throughout this process.

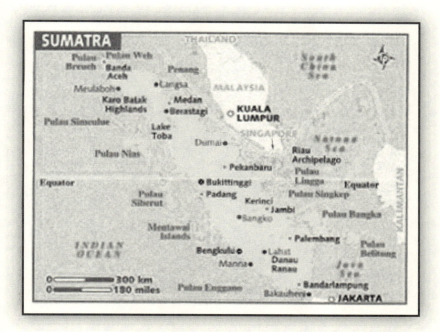

SAMOSIR ISLAND ON LAKE TOBA

BUKIT LAWANG

BATAK WEDDING

RICE PRESENTS

SUNARYO & FAMILY

LEPER BEGGAR

BANDA ACEH DISTROYED BY THE 2004 TSUNAMI

CHAPTER 9

Summing Up

At the critical age of sixty-three our Csipogo had an important financial decision to make. To continue working until the compulsory retirement age of sixty-five or retire early. The company has been downsizing and encouraged early retirement by offering $50,000 packages.

I can't save $50,000 in two years. I might as well take the package and retire now, he thought.

We have our mortgage paid for, and we have our summer cottage in the Okanagan. I have a company pension, Registered Retirement Saving Plan (RRSP) and Old Age Security pension and we have savings in stocks and bonds that pay dividend. We have enough to live in reasonable comfort in old age and help our sons with down payments to enable them to purchase their own homes, Csipogo reasoned.

I am blessed with speaking two languages, and in the remaining time given to me, I might be able to translate some worthwhile Hungarian novels into English, learn to play some musical instrument, play golf in the Okanagan in summer time and take winter vacations in San Jose del Cabo, Mexico, he continued on dreamily.

Csipogo drew up a financial roadmap to run a balanced budget. He gave $50,000 to each of his three sons. The three boys were all happily married to three wonderful girls. "I love these girls more than I love my own sons," Csipogo was often heard saying. He budgeted $1200 per month for his wife to run the household expenses and $500/month for personal expenses. It looked like a very reasonable plan.

But the external environment has gone through a massive change, from the time when he entered the workforce. The rot has permeated every level of society from top to bottom. He started out in a time of truly *conservative* social credit government in Alberta, which believed that alcohol and gambling were evil. Drugs were nonexistent on the street level. There were no home invasions, and people could leave their homes unlocked; there was no need for iron bars in windows. People took pride in their workmanship, and there was a reasonable equality in the pay scales. As an engineer in training, he started out with a salary of $500 per month, and the CEO of the company earned roughly $5,000 per month and a modest bonus if warranted. This was a reasonable difference for increased responsibilities. But greed and corruption entered the scene in a big way; it entered the governments, businesses, and individuals. Social conscience started to erode. The rich class deluded themselves that they deserved the riches earned on the backs of others; after all this is a capitalistic society. Socialism became a dirty word. Governments spent the public money recklessly. The business community turned up more crooks like Bernie Madoff than philanthropists like Warren Buffett and Bill Gates. Governments started to sell off the publicly owned Crown Corporations as if they owned them under the pretext that private ownership was more efficient and cut-throat competition of airlines, telephone companies, hydro companies, gas companies, car insurance companies, and railways was good for the public. Governments spent public funds to bail out mismanaged corporations. Private debts were turned into public debts on a massive scale. Sales tax on corporations was transferred to the public as consumption tax. Every activity had to be commercialized. Manufacturing was hollowed out by greed; companies started moving to China and India to take advantage of lower wages. Today telephone help lines in Canada are manned from India and the Philippines. Bankruptcies progressed from individuals and corporations to entire countries failing: Mexico, Argentina, Ireland, Portugal, Greece . . .

Gambling crept in on all levels. You can now make bets whether the stock market will go up or it will go down. You can buy stocks on margins of 10 percent down. Worthless bonds were packaged and sold as blue-chip investment, with the blessings of banks and rating agencies. Governments on all levels draw revenues from the pipe dreams of people of hitting it big without working for it. There are over-the-counter lotteries of all kinds, gambling casinos in nearly every municipality that are open twenty-four hours a day, gambling on the internet right from your home to gamble away your home. Gambling addiction, just like alcohol addiction and drug addiction, is hitting families with devastating consequences. People get divorced, and some commit suicide when they can no longer pay their debts. But debt is readily offered by the banks; at 19 percent interest their credit cards are their most profitable business.

Gambling is a slow and insidious disease. It starts with small bets, to get that feeling of '*rush*' that comes with winning. But with time, the bets increase, and when the losses start to accumulate, the chase begins to win it back. But you can't win it back. Casinos are not designed to lose; they are designed to win. It started slowly with Carolyn, on vacations in holiday resorts. It was not yet dangerous; Csipogo was earning good wages and occasional losses had no serious and lasting consequences. But it was quite something else after retirement. The family had a budgetary constraint.

The first shock came when Carolyn presented Csipogo with a $35,000 credit card debt. He paid it off by taking a line of credit against their home. That is what Carolyn wanted. "It is my money too," she said.

But when you pay off a credit card debt, the banks will offer you a higher credit card limit. And the next time the credit card debt came in at $50,000.

Now Csipogo was confronted with a situation that potentially endangered the very financial foundation of the family. The bank will gladly increase the home line of credit. In the low interest environment of 3 percent this was still supportable with paying the interest only, but the bank now had a permanent hold on the home. But what will happen when the interest rates rise to the more normal level of 6 percent or 10 percent? Now the family cash flow would become negative and all assets could be swallowed up by the debt. Csipogo decided to increase the home line of credit to $100,000 against his better judgment, hoping that the problem will somehow disappear. But gambling addiction does not easily release its victim. Every time they are depressed or upset by something or with someone, they slip back to it and it gets progressively worse. All logical reasoning vanishes.

"I know you don't like talking about it, but you must stop your gambling habit, to avoid breaking up your family unit. Your husband is dealing with a severe health issue. Battling cancer is enough stress on him, and he doesn't need the additional burden of dealing with your gambling losses," Carolyn's sister Ester, warned her.

"I know . . . I must stop" Carolyn said at a near whisper.

The Okanagen Valley stretches from Osoyoos at the United States border north to Vernon. The valley is dry and has a semidesert climate. It is blessed with three beautiful fresh water lakes stretching for the valley's entire 150 miles length: Osoyoos Lake, Skaha Lake, and Okanagen Lake. Beloved by thousands of visitors and inhabitants alike for the unparalleled variety of its climate and landscape, the Okanagen Valley offers something for everyone: orchards, vineyards, mountains, valleys, lakes, ski slopes and trails. This is truly one of the most desirable locales in British Columbia and quite possibly in the entire world.

After passing through the arid Osoyoos and Oliver regions and head north up the valley, one finds hundreds of orchards and vineyards, evidence of some of the best fruit and vegetable growing land in the world. There are more than sixty provincial parks, and dozens and dozens of recreation sites. The Okanagan's open terrain makes it ideal for hiking and backpacking, with little or no bushwhacking required. There are thirty-seven golf courses scattered between Osoyoos and Vernon. Kelowna Springs Golf Course has seven natural spring-fed lakes, and more than a thousand apple trees grow on the fairways of Harvest Golf Club. Gallagher's Canyon Golf & Country Club straddles Gallagher's Canyon, through which a river runs. Predator Ridge Golf Resort near Vernon has not one, but two 18 holes courses and a world famous Crystal Wellness Center. Vernon boasts with another famous golf course, the Riser, designed by Freddie Couples. And in the winter Apex, Big White, and Silver Star ski resorts offer skiers the best powder snow available anywhere.

The major population centers are Osoyoos at the south end, Penticton and Kelowna in the middle and Vernon at the north end.

It is here that Csipogo purchased a half acre recreational lot at Killiney Beach on the West side of Okanagan Lake prior to leaving for Indonesia in 1991. It was a second tier lot with a beautiful view of Okanagan Lake, with visibility all the way to Vernon. It was probably the best purchase he has ever made in his life, not just for monetary reasons, but for the enjoyment it provided to him, his family, and friends.

It was really his youngest son Paul who made the decision.

"Let's buy it Dad! It is so beautiful and peaceful here."

It was for sale by owner. When Csipogo phoned her, she turned out to be an elderly Hungarian lady, who lived in Penticton. She was more than pleased that it is a countryman of hers who is buying the land.

Another gift was the fact that John Carr, one of his engineering colleague and soccer-playing friend, owned the water front lot below him. It was actually John who told him about the lot being for sale.

"If I had the money, I would buy it myself," John told him.

The lot was on a gently sloping hill and was treed largely by Ponderosa pine. It had no road yet into the lot, and after returning from Indonesia, Csipogo contacted Wayne Watson, a local contractor with heavy equipment, to cut a road and level a flat landscape large enough for a future cottage. It was done on a handshake and trust basis.

"Go ahead and give me the bill when you are done," Csipogo told Wayne. All future work was done on that basis, and Csipogo had never been disappointed.

The lot looked to the east, and Csipogo's greatest pleasure was to sit and read a book, facing the early morning rising sun. And when the full moon rose above the east side mountain top and shone a bright light on the water the full width of the lake, it was a marvel to behold. This was such a favorite spot that Karen, his youngest son's wife, placed a plaque on the ground, under the chair.

Csipogo's friends, Miki and Ann, at this time, also lived in Vancouver; in fact they were the first to move here from Edmonton, and they enjoyed coming to the lot. Miki loved to sit in the same chair in the mornings and advise Csipogo what to do and how to do it. Paul came visiting from Edmonton and Tamas and Judit, his other close Hungarian friends, came from as far as Toronto to have a vacation in a trailer.

In the beginning, they had no water yet on the property, and they had to bring water in buckets from John's property below. It reminded Csipogo of his early youth when they carried water jugs from the nearby artesian well in Hungary and played dirty tricks on the neighborhood girls, emptying their water jugs in mock Indian attacks.

They had no outhouse either. There was a His and Hers on Killiney Beach, some five hundred meters down the road. Csipogo and Miki often wondered if they can make it or have to rush and hide behind a Ponderosa tree along the way. They always carried '*papel higienico*' with them, just in case. So, it was no small wonder that the next most urgent job was to build an outhouse.

And what a building it turned out to be. It was a marvel of engineering and ecological design. Miki was sitting in his usual chair and was telling Csipogo what to do during the construction.

"Have you ever built and outhouse?" Ann asked Miki.

"Yes, I did, on Lake Wabamun . . . remember?" Miki retorted.

The building had to face the lake and the location for it was selected a little way uphill . . . but not too far. The door was built to half height, to allow the occupants have a view of the lake. And the seat had to be comfortable and large enough for both his and hers. It was a place for day dreaming, for enjoyment of the lake view, and to watch people walking by and not picking up after their dogs.

The next project was to bring water to the lot, no more carrying of buckets uphill. And the irrigation enabled the next development, planting of fruit trees and grape vines.

"Next we have to get rid of lanterns," Miki said.

"I agree," Csipogo stated, and a BC Hydro pole was installed. Now they had nearly every comfort of life: a comfortable trailer, water and electricity.

"The ultimate comfort would be not to have to walk to the outhouse in the middle of the night. We need a septic field for the trailer," Karen suggested.

Karen and Csipogo's grandchildren had a valid reason for not wanting to go to the outhouse in the middle of the night: the neighborhood bear.

This bear was a nuisance in more ways than one. He was a threat to the table grapes during the ripening season in September. The grape vines were conveniently planted hip high behind the stone wall that was built to hold back the hill and for the benefit of the bear standing on his hind feet and reaching out with his front paws. The first year's harvest was more his than Csipogo's. And at one time, on one of his trips to the lake, Csipogo forgot to empty his cooler and left it overnight, fully loaded on the picnic table outside. It had Carolyn's roast beef and mashed potatoes, ham sandwiches, various gourmet cheeses, pastry, and a whole rod of spicy Hungarian salami in it. The next morning the cooler was empty, except for the Hungarian salami. The bear bit into it, but he obviously didn't fancy spicy Hungarian paprika.

Now, after nearly twenty years of looking after the land, it yielded seedless table grapes, peaches, apricots, nectarines, gala

FIND A PLACE TO CALL HOME

apples, and Italian plums in great profusion, and there is simply no other greater satisfaction in this whole world than tasting fully ripened produce from your own trees.

It is this recreational paradise that will now have to be sold to pay off the accumulating gambling debt.

Vancouver, British Columbia has the largest and most beautifully constructed outdoor saltwater swimming pool in Canada. Csipogo was driving Phoenix, his five-year-old grandson there, for an afternoon frolicking in the sun.

"It is very important to learn to swim," Csipogo was lecturing his grandson.

Phoenix was very quiet for awhile and then blurted out something that took his grandfather's breath away.

"Grandpa, do you know what else is very important?"

"No. What is?"

"It is important to have a home."

Csipogo was stunned where the five year old child got this idea . . . and then he noticed a homeless person sleeping on the sidewalk.

SUMMER COTTAGE IN THE OKANAGEN